Tales and Whispers

short stories and personal quotes

Régis Auffray

BOOKS BY RÉGIS AUFFRAY

Born Again: The Limericks of Régis

Glimpses

Through the Mist

Tales and Whispers

ACKNOWLEDGEMENTS

I wish to extend my thanks to all of those who have continually encouraged me to write and to share my writing endeavors with others in the form of this book of short stories and personal quotes. You know who you are.

I am also very thankful to my friend, writer and author, Lena Kovadlo for her professional assistance in the formatting and final presentation of this project.

TABLE OF CONTENTS

PART ONE – TALES

Stories from Régis...

DEAD MAN DANCING

When Mr. Reginald ("Rocky" to his few close friends) Livingstone woke up on November 1st, he was dead.

He'd had that recurring nightmare again. Ever since he could remember, the nightmare had been a regular visitor to his sleep. In it, a veiled shadow was chasing him and, just as it was about to reveal its face, he always woke up.

Mr. Livingstone decided that he was dead when he got out of bed. He had been in denial he said to himself. He had been dead for some time. Now upon admitting it, he felt as though he were floating. He had been lying to himself, he thought; and now this huge burden of guilt was removed. It was strangely exhilarating; scary but freeing at the same time. It left a bittersweet but not unpleasant sensation in the pit of his stomach.

He went through his usual routine. He began to rationalize. Routine was his life so he couldn't very well give it up just because he was dead now could he?

- Push-ups (50)
- Floss teeth
- Shave

- Push-ups (another 50)
- Floss teeth
- Brush teeth
- Get dressed
- Coffee
- Put on shoes
- Pick up briefcase
- Punch in alarm code
- Push button on remote control for garage door
- Open front door
- Lock door
- Get in car
- Back out of garage
- Push button on remote control to close garage door
- Engage transmission
- Drive to office

All this he did while dead and he found that he enjoyed it very much as his dead brain ticked "check" after each item on the routine list. He found that he could skip some items and nothing bad happened. So he skipped a lot of them. Yes, being dead was very freeing.

As usual, Mr. Livingstone drove carefully but he found that, contrary to his usual fear of fender benders and such, he was completely relaxed and rather enjoying the drive. As he got closer to the downtown core, the traffic became more and more congested. Soon, it was at a standstill. Mr. Livingstone was not bothered by this at all. He was dead. He moved his dead body to the music. He wished he had some Grateful Dead tunes but Led Zeppelin's "Stairway to Heaven" seemed appropriate enough and as he listened to the fast part, he felt uplifted and full of self-confidence. He could see the office building where he worked just ahead. "Foundation Fidelity Financial – In Us You Trust," flashed the sign. Oh yeah, the good old FFF. Man, he could think of some words to fit those initials. Normally, he would chase those nasty thoughts from his mind. His mother had always said to chase away the devil thoughts with Jesus thoughts. Well now, he was dead and to hell with morals and long dead mothers who had constantly reminded him of how unworthy he was.

The traffic was not moving at all. After some minutes, as the music to Led Zeppelin's famous hit came to an end, Mr. Livingstone thought that a walk would do him good. Dead people don't need cars anyway, he thought. He turned off the engine, took his briefcase and got out of the car. It was amazingly noisy and the rather frigid air was full of fumes but he was not bothered by any of this at all. Normally, he would be thinking of pollution and his health and global warming and the vanishing ozone layer and the melting polar ice caps and... and... and... But now? Ha! He could not have felt better. This dead to the world thing had something to it. It was very energizing. As he walked away from his car, the drivers behind him began to honk and shout curses at him as they activated their middle finger. He was not oblivious to them. He rather basked in all the attention given him. Wow, finally, some recognition! I am stirring my surroundings for a change. Look at me! I am dead! Whee! I am free! He waved at the furious commuters with a beatific smile on his face as he walked across the lanes of traffic in the direction of the office tower.

Mr. Livingstone entered the building and took the elevator to the twenty-second floor. He was late by some twenty-five minutes but he did not care. His colleagues stared in unbelief as he sauntered past their glassed-in cubicles. He smiled his serene smile. Had they never seen an unshaven man in pajamas before? Okay, so he'd forgotten his shoes. Had they not ever heard of how it was much better for one's health to liberate one's toes, particularly when one was dead? Most likely not. But they would learn. Soon. They would have to if they wanted to survive. They'd have to follow his example.

He walked past Merle Bosman's office. Merle – Mr. Livingstone was sure it was the first time he'd ever dared think of him as Merle and not as Mr. Bosman – the director of personnel, did not look pleased at all. In fact, he looked genuinely about to have a conniption. Mr. Livingstone thought of how he loved that word. Conniption was a good word. It could mean a lot. He'd never caused anyone to have a conniption before. Being dead gave him a new sense of power. At last he was making a difference around him. He was being noticed.

"Conniption! Conniption! You're having a conniption, Merle!" He laughed the hearty laugh of a truly happy man.

Bosman was gesticulating wildly at Mr. Livingstone. The latter smiled at him and entered his stall. From the corner of his eye, he could see Merle trying to get his attention and waving him over. Mr. Livingstone ignored him. He put down his briefcase. He stared at the logo on the paperweight on his desk. "Foundation Fidelity Financial – In Us You Trust" read the inscription in shining letters. How he hated that damned paperweight. Oops, had he actually said the "d" word? What would mother say? He chuckled. "Who gives a flying futon?" he thought. "I am dead."

Merle was banging on the glass partition now and emphatically waving Mr. Livingstone over to him. Mr. Livingstone slowly made his way into Merle's office smiling his serene, senile smile all the while.

"What the hell do you think you're doing, Livingstone?" screamed the director of personnel. "Have you completely lost it?"   •

"You could say that," replied Mr. Livingstone very calmly. "I'm dead." I've bought the farm as they say. Well actually, I sold the farm but that was in my past life when I was still alive. Yes indeed I have kicked the bucket. I'm pushing up daisies. My expiry date's come due. I'm as dead as a doornail. I've cashed in my chips. I'm as dead as a drowned bluebottle fly in a pitcher of milk. And you know what? I love every wonderful moment of it. You should try it. You'd be way better off dead anyway. In fact, you are dead Merle. You are a dead man!"

"Is that a threat, Livingstone? Are you threatening me?" demanded Merle.

Mr. Livingstone smiled.

"Is that all, Merle?" he asked. And before the incensed Merle could respond, Mr. Livingstone turned away and walked slowly back to his workplace.

He went to his desk. He picked up the hated paperweight. It felt good in his hands, quite heavy but not too much so. Like a baseball. He looked into Merle's office. The latter was on the telephone. Mr. Livingstone lifted the paperweight and, with all the strength of his newly acquired freedom in death, hurled it at the computer screen on Merle's desk. With great fracas, the paperweight smashed through the glass partition, shattered the computer monitor's screen and imbedded itself neatly there, the shining logo proclaiming, "Foundation Fidelity Financial – In Us You Trust."

Merle was visibly shaking. He had dropped the telephone and stood completely still. He appeared unreservedly horrified.

Mr. Livingstone felt an ethereal sense of elation and well-being. He saw the policemen coming and went to greet them.

"Good day, gentlemen," he said. "I am the dead man you are looking for."

The police put him in handcuffs. His colleagues stared at him through their glass boxes. He could see they were dead but they had not yet grasped the concept.

"You're all dead!" he screamed hysterically and yet, seemingly joyfully. "You just don't realize how wonderful it is to embrace death." Look at me! Look at how happy I am! I am free! Whee!"

That night while Mr. Livingstone soundly slept the sleep of the dead in his padded cell, the shadowy figure came into his dream again. This time however, it had time to remove the veil from its face and Mr. Livingstone was thrilled to see that it was none other than himself; he smiled and went back to the peaceful sleep of the dead.

THE SANDMAN

(some adult language)

The first time Mike heard about the famous (or, perhaps infamous would be a better word) lotion, he was listening to some of his friends who had gathered inside the covered shelter on the sports field near the school. He had been thinking that they were making fun of him behind his back. Since Jenny, his first real girlfriend had moved away six days ago, Mike had not been his old self and his fair weather friends seemed to have been increasingly keeping their distance. In this case however, Mike soon realized that they were not in the least bit concerned about him, at least not at the moment. He had sneaked up behind the shed and hidden among the thick elderberry shrubs so that they had no idea he was nearby. Ronnie Bowles was doing most of the talking.

"You guys should see what this stuff has done to my mom. You know what a pain in the ass she can be. Well, since she's been taking this shit, she just leaves me alone. No more questions about what I was doing last night, no more hassles about my room, no more of that crap about my homework. It's just awesome. It's like she doesn't care anymore. She's just like she's, uh, happy, you know? As a matter of fact, when I left the house this morning, she didn't even come out of her room, it's like she wasn't even there, you know?"

Kevin Crawford, the leader of the group, looked a little bewildered. "Do you mean your old lady's finally seen the light? Like, she's actually letting you have a life? Man, I can't believe it. She's got to be the most absolute bitch of a mom."

Ronnie replied emphatically, "You better believe it. My troubles are over, man! Let's go over to the arcade and afterwards, we can see if there's a party somewhere. It's not like I got to go home or anything."

And on it went for another minute or two as Mike's friends started walking across the field. For a moment, he thought about joining them but he changed his mind when he thought about the math test he had to take the next morning.

Mike waited until his buddies were out of sight and then he walked across the school yard toward his home. By now, his dad would be back home from an after work session of playing golf with his buddies from the office and, if he was lucky, his mom would have settled down to watch a rented video and she would leave him and his father to their own endeavours for the evening. His mom had never really recovered from the death of his sister some seven years back. Not that anybody could have done anything about what happened at the time. Some psycho decides to begin his life mission on the wrong day at the wrong time and, so long, sis; it was nice knowing you. Meagan had been sixteen at the time and she'd been the best big sister a ten year old kid brother could ever have. God, he'd gone to enough counselling sessions to get the pain and anger out of himself. Still, he thought, if that son of a bitch was ever found, he'd never make it to the slammer because he, Michael James Achton would be the first in line to blow the bastard away, one way or another. Well, it would be best not to think of that at the moment. This was not one of the best days that he'd had in a while.

The next morning dawned with Mike up well before the sun. This was his best time to study; to "cram," actually. He knew he would do well on this math test although he still hated that vague feeling of unease he always felt before an exam. There was always that little voice from somewhere in the uncharted reaches of his mind that kept repeating over and over that this time, he just might blow it.

Three hours later, Mike came out of the exam room. He felt confident that he had done well. As he walked out of the school yard, he saw several people lined up behind an old beat-up station wagon on the vacant site of the old, now abandoned drive-in theatre. He didn't have to come much closer for a look to know that Mr. Promiser was back in town selling his wares. As he came nearer, he could hear him,

"Yes, ladies and gentlemen, this here lotion is a wonder of wonders. It'll cure anything from ague to zits, from A to Zee, ladies and gentlemen, from A to Zee. It'll pick you up if you're down, and, for you boys and girls in school, why it'll even make you smarter. Come forward, ladies and gentlemen and get your free sample. I see that a lot of you folks who took samples the last time are back for more. Well, no more free samples for you but, have I got a deal for you! See this here bottle? For a mere ten dollars plus tax of course, it's yours. And look at the size! There's a lot of happiness bottled up in there folks. And look at the shape! Why it'll fit like a charm just about anywhere you'd want to put it. Step forward folks and let me, Abe Promiser, also known as The Sandman, take away your aches and pains and give you a taste of heaven. That's right, honey. Come right on up. My, my but you sure are a pretty thing ain't you...? And on he went, barely stopping his spiel while he handed out bottles and took in money.

Abe Promiser had been selling wares from the back of his battered 1972 Ford station wagon ever since Mike could remember. He had been nicknamed "The Sandman" because, after crossing the desert on his way into town, his clothes, his car and his merchandise were covered with the grainy matter. It seemed the sand had become his trademark. Although Mr. Promiser's sales had never been brisk, he kept coming back month after month, year after year. Nobody knew much about him. He never stayed in town for more than a few hours. He had never taken a meal at the sole local diner and he had never stayed at the town's only motel. Nobody knew where his home was and most suspected that he didn't have one.

As Mike watched, he could not help but notice that the scene today was unlike any he'd ever observed during The Sandman's previous visits. People were jostling each other in their eagerness to make a purchase and, Mike realized with mounting curiosity, everyone was buying one thing and one thing only: The Sandman's latest concoction, the miraculous lotion. Over the buzz of animated conversation, he could hear Abe Promiser:

"You can smoke it, you can toke it. You can put it on your nose, you can put it on your toes; hey, folks, you can even eat it if you so desire. It'll make you high; it'll make you fly, why it'll even improve your love life. Come on folks, before The Sandman, that would be me folks, runs out..." And he laughed.

Mike turned away and started towards home. Most of the people he passed on the street were coming back from their recent encounter with The Sandman and they were not talkative. Each seemed intent on going somewhere as quickly as possible, as if each had a secret tryst, a lot like minors with bootlegged liquor heading for the river on a Friday night. Mike's greetings were seldom acknowledged save for a few grunts now and then.

When Mike came into his yard, he was dismayed to see the family car still parked in front of the garage. His father never missed a day of work and he seemed never to get sick. Mike let himself into the house and yelled out, "Anybody home? Mom, are you there?"

No answer. Mike started up the stairs towards his parents' bedroom. The door was wide open but the curtains were drawn and the light was weak. Mike could hear snoring. It had to be his dad. As his eyes grew accustomed to the dim surroundings, he realized that both of his parents were naked. Mike had never seen his parents in a state of undress but here they were, both of them as naked as patrons of a nudist colony on the first warm day of spring.

Shocked, Mike turned around to leave but as he did so, he tripped on one of his father's boots, fell against the bedside table, knocking the lamp to the floor with a crash. His father sat up in bed. He seemed not to comprehend what was happening.

"Why son, what are you doing here?" his father asked, his voice thick and his speech somewhat slurred.

"I could ask you the same thing, Dad. Why aren't you at work? It's two o'clock in the afternoon!"

"Aw, son, chill out! Work! Work! Work! That's all you can think of. A person's got to enjoy life once in a while, you know? Take a load off, relax, smell the coffee...or is it the roses? Whatever..."

"But what about your job? Did you call in sick? What's Mr. Bosman going to think?"

"Relax, son. Bosman didn't go to work either. Me and the rest of the guys showed up at the plant but it was locked tight. So we went and got some of that new lotion from The Sandman and, you could say, the rest is history. Me and your mom here are just gonna take it easy for a while. Why don't you try some of that stuff? There's a bottle on the counter downstairs. Help yourself, son. It'll help you relax, you know? Just lie back and unwind, smell... the roses... nothing else really matters... it...doesn't...really...matterrr...zzz..."

Mike watched as his father's eyes closed and he started snoring again. His mom hadn't moved at all. For all he knew, she could be dead. He could feel the old anger like a waking beast stirring from deep within himself and that voice again, saying things it shouldn't, it mustn't...

Mike went downstairs. He was hungry. He opened the refrigerator. The smell that greeted his nostrils was enough to gag him and the mouldy leftovers were enough to quell any hunger pangs that might have survived the aromatic-visual experience he had just witnessed. He looked at the bottle on the counter. "I wonder what it tastes like?" he thought. "I suppose there would be no harm in trying just a little. I mean; the old man's right. I have been a little uptight lately."

He twisted the cap off the bottle and as he did so, he noticed it was gritty. He looked more closely. Sure enough there was Abe Promiser's trademark: sand, several grains of it along the rim of the bottle. He sniffed at the liquid inside. It didn't smell like anything. He put his index finger inside and touched the liquid. An immediate tingling sensation began to spread from the tip of his finger to the rest of his hand and up the length of his right arm. Wow! That was some powerful stuff! He dipped his finger into the bottle again and this time, brought his finger to the tip of his tongue. The result was immediate and explosive, certainly unlike anything he'd ever experienced. Sure, he'd had a few beers in the past and he had sneaked some of his father's rye whiskey, but this was nothing like that. In fact, Mike had to admit that he didn't have the words to describe this new sensation. He lifted the bottle to his lips and took a swallow. As he lowered the bottle, his pupils dilated and the sunlight coming through the curtains became a myriad of intersecting rainbows while the dust motes floating through them became planets and galaxies and...

...The bottle fell to the floor but Mike did not bend down to pick it up. As the liquid poured out on the shiny vinyl flooring, Mike stared at it. He saw a river flowing from the bottle towards his left foot. There was something floating on the surface. Now he bent down for a closer look. It was sand, of course. What else could it be? Sand! Just more fucking sand! What did you expect when you had dealings with The Sandman? Still what was it about sand? Sand! Sand! Sand!

The word just wouldn't go away! Why? Why? And then, slowly, like a figure emerging from the mist, he saw Meagan's body; he saw her face and it came to him and the awfulness of the thought took his breath away. The investigators had found sand among Meagan's clothing and they had never been able to figure out where it had come from. Now he knew! He knew who it was! And for a moment, the angry beast within him tried to rise. But it was tired and it didn't seem all that important somehow. As Mike watched the liquid continue to flow from the bottle, his toes began to vanish beneath the surface of the river. He looked up and stared ahead. The rainbows and the planets were beautiful and it didn't matter anymore...nothing really mattered except this feeling...this slipping away...didn't matter...didn't... ...nothing mattered.

Outside, in the distance, The Sandman ranted on, "You can shake it, and you can bake it. Inside, outside; it'll make you prance, it'll make you dance. Come on folks! Step right up and let The Sandman make you fly...oh my yes! Ain't you a pretty one! Step right on up here honey, come on, there's no need to be shy now...

MARKI ET LE GÉANT

Il était une fois dans un pays loin d'ici un petit garçon qui s'appelait Marki. Il habitait dans un village près d'une grande forêt. On croyait que la forêt était enchantée mais personne n'en était vraiment certain car tout le monde disait qu'il était impossible d'y aller à cause du géant Maxibottes. Ce géant était appelé ainsi à cause de ses énormes bottes rouges qu'il portait fièrement.

Le géant Maxibottes avait un grand château non loin du village à la lisière de la forêt mystérieuse. De son château, Maxibottes pouvait voir tous ceux qui osaient s'approcher de la forêt, et jamais il n'avait laissé personne y entrer.

Les habitants du village dont je vous parle étaient des paysans qui gagnaient leur pain en cultivant la terre des environs. Ils travaillaient du matin au soir à s'occuper de leurs récoltes et de leurs animaux. Ils auraient sûrement été heureux si Maxibottes les avait laissés à leurs travaux quotidiens. Mais le méchant géant s'amusait à faire du mal aux pauvres gens du village.

De temps en temps, sans raison apparente, Maxibottes sortait de son château et choisissait un champ d'avoine, d'orge, ou de blé. Il y courrait à droite et à gauche et ainsi détruisait la récolte espérée d'un pauvre paysan. Les villageois terrifiés, cachés dans leurs maisons, pouvaient entendre ses éclats de rire. Ils savaient bien que cela signifiait qu'un d'entre eux venait de perdre sa récolte. Ils priaient que le champ en question ne fut pas le leur.

Comme je l'ai mentionné plus tôt, il habitait dans ce village un petit garçon nommé Marki. Marki aimait observer tout ce qu'il apercevait autour de lui. Il pouvait rester des heures à écouter les chants des oiseaux, à regarder une paire de fauvettes bâtir leur nid, ou à observer les nuages dans le ciel. Il aimait beaucoup sentir la pluie sur son visage. L'hiver, quand la neige tombait, Marki, étendu sur le sol, adorait laisser les flocons le couvrir. Quand le vent soufflait, il aimait courir dehors pour le regarder jouer dans les champs de blé y faisant des ondulations qui ressemblaient aux vagues de la mer. Marki aimait penser que le champ était un océan où il partirait bientôt dans son bateau imaginaire.

Les actions de Maxibottes faisait beaucoup de peine à Marki. Il ne comprenait pas pourquoi ce géant pouvait être aussi méchant sans provocation. Souvent, avant de s'endormir le soir, Marki priait, demandant à Dieu comment il pourrait venir en aide à ses parents et aux autres habitants de la région.

Une nuit, Marki fit un rêve étrange. Dans le rêve, il se trouvait dans une sombre forêt et il parlait avec deux femmes qu'il n'avait jamais vues auparavant. Lorsqu'il se réveilla, il se rappela que sa conversation avec les deux femmes avait fait allusion au géant Maxibottes.

Quelques jours plus tard, comme était son habitude vers le coucher du soleil, le géant Maxibottes sortit de son château. Cette fois, il se dirigea vers la ferme des parents de Marki et commença à écraser la récolte qui s'y trouvait. Ses éclats de rire faisaient trembler les villageois terrifiés, et ses enjambées faisaient aussi trembler le sol. Le géant s'amusa ainsi jusqu'à ce que la lune fût déjà haute dans le ciel, puis il rentra chez lui.

Le lendemain matin, Marki et sa famille se rendirent compte que le géant avait complètement anéanti leur récolte. Il fallait recommencer et espérer que ni l'hiver ni le géant ne reviendraient trop vite afin de pouvoir faire pousser une autre récolte de blé.

Ce jour-là, Marki regardait vers la forêt lointaine quand il lui vint une pensée. Il se rappela son rêve. Soudain, il fut persuadé qu'il devait se rendre dans la forêt mystérieuse. Ce soir-là, au souper, il fit part de ses projets à ses parents. Ni son père ni sa mère ne purent comprendre pourquoi il voulait aller dans la forêt.

"Tu sais bien qu'il est impossible d'aller dans la forêt. Maxibottes ne laisse passer personne." lui dit son père.

"Mais oui, mon garçon." continua sa mère. "Tous ceux qui ont essayé d'aller dans la forêt ne sont jamais revenus. Ne pense plus à de telles sottises!"

Lorsqu'il fut dans son lit, avant de s'endormir, Marki réfléchit de nouveau. Il se rendit compte du fait que le géant ne sortait jamais faire ses dégâts quand le soleil était haut dans le ciel. Pourquoi? La réponse était simple: Maxibottes devait dormir l'après-midi. Marki se décida. Le lendemain, il irait dans la forêt enchantée.

Le jour suivant, lorsque le soleil fut à son zénith, Marki partit sans que personne ne puisse le voir. Il se dirigea tout droit vers la forêt enchantée. Bien sûr, il devait passer devant le château du méchant géant. Il serait faux de dire que Marki n'avait pas peur. Plus il s'approchait du château, plus il pensait aux gens du village qui avaient essayé d'aller dans la forêt. Aucun d'entre eux n'était jamais revenu. Que leur était-il arrivé? Plus d'une fois, Marki était sur le point de retourner chez lui. Mais chaque fois qu'il allait faire demi-tour, il se rappelait son rêve. Dans sa tête, il voyait les deux femmes mystérieuses qui semblaient l'encourager à continuer. C'est ainsi qu'il fut bientôt sous les arbres de la forêt enchantée.

Une fois arrivé dans la forêt, Marki se demanda où il devait aller. Il n'eut pas à attendre longtemps. Tout à coup, il vit un sentier devant lui. Il le suivit et peu après, il se trouva devant une petite chaumière. Il frappa à la porte. Presque immédiatement, la porte fut ouverte.

"Bonjour, Marki." lui dit la belle femme qui avait ouvert la porte.

"Bonjour, madame." dit Marki en la saluant. "Comment savez-vous mon nom?" demanda Marki.

"Ma soeur et moi, nous t'attendons depuis un bon moment." lui répondit la femme.

"Qui êtes-vous?" demanda Marki.

"Je m'appelle Jolicristal. J'habite ici avec ma soeur Jobelle." lui dit la femme mystérieuse. La voici."

Marki fut émerveillé par la beauté de cette nouvelle venue.

"Jobelle, je te présente Marki." dit Jolicristal.

"Enchantée, Marki." dit Jobelle.

Jolicristal continua: "Nous sommes des fées. Nous savons que Maxibottes vous fait de méchantes choses depuis longtemps. Mais jusqu'ici, personne n'a pu parvenir à nous trouver. Tu es le premier à se rendre compte que le géant a un point faible. Tous les jours, l'après-midi, il s'endort."

"Que dois-je faire pour débarrasser ce méchant géant de la région?" demanda Marki.

"Quand le géant se réveille, il boit toujours une chope de bière qu'il garde à côté de son lit." continua Jobelle. "Nous avons préparé une tisane magique. Si tu parviens à faire que le géant la boive, il perdra ses pouvoirs."

"Vous voulez me dire que je dois entrer dans le château de Maxibottes et que je dois aller dans sa chambre?" s'écria Marki.

"C'est exactement ce que tu dois faire." lui dit Jolicristal.

"Voici la tisane magique, Marki. Dépêche-toi! Le géant va se réveiller bientôt. Bon courage!" dit la fée Jobelle.

"Merci, mesdames," répondit Marki. "À bientôt, j'espère."

Aussi vite que possible, Marki se rendit au château de Maxibottes. Il entra par la porte ouverte. Il n'eut pas de difficulté à trouver le géant car il pouvait entendre ses ronflements. Dans la chambre du géant, Marki ajouta la tisane magique à la bière. Puis, il se cacha derrière la porte pour voir ce qui allait se passer.

Peu après, Maxibottes soupira longuement, il grogna, et se réveilla. Il s'étira et regarda autour de lui. Derrière la porte, Marki, tremblait de frayeur. Maxibottes grogna encore une fois puis il prit la chope dans sa main. En un seul coup, il but la bière et aussi, sans le savoir, la tisane des fées.

Tout à coup, le géant perdit sa forme effrayante. Il devint de plus en plus petit. En quelques instants, il ne fut pas plus grand que le père de Marki.

Dehors, le ciel s'était recouvert de nuages noirs. Une violente tempête avait apporté du tonnerre, des éclairs et une pluie abondante sur la région.

Marki sortit de sa cachette derrière la porte. Le "géant" qui n'était plus un géant lui dit, "Salut, Marki!" C'est toi qui as fait que je suis enfin libre du sort qu'un méchant sorcier m'avait jeté il y a si longtemps. Merci, grand merci!"

"C'est mon plaisir," répondit Marki.

Maxibottes libéra ceux qui étaient prisonniers dans son château et à peine Marki, Maxibottes et les prisonniers furent-ils sortis que le château s'écroula. Tout à coup, ils virent dans le ciel un phénomène incroyable. Un grand arc composé de violet, d'indigo, de bleu, de vert, de jaune, d'orange, et de rouge se trouvait devant eux.

"On dirait un arc dans le ciel!" s'écria Marki.

"Oui, tu as bien raison." répondit Maxibottes. "C'est un arc-en-ciel. C'est le signe qui indique que je suis enfin libre du méchant sortilège duquel je suis victime depuis si longtemps."

Peu après, Maxibottes changea de nom. Il portait toujours ses bottes rouges alors on l'appela, Monsieur Rougebottes.

Autant que je sache, Marki, sa famille, et Monsieur Rougebottes habitent toujours dans leur pays lointain; et de temps en temps, c'est avec grand plaisir que Marki reçoit la visite des fées Jobelle et Jolicristal.

LIKE FATHER, LIKE SON

(some adult content)

Edward Bossiner looked east across the city. It was only four o'clock in the afternoon but already, blue dusk was spreading her skirts over the streets below and the neighbouring skyscrapers. Edward, Eddy to his friends, sipped from a generous tumbler of well-aged, expensive whiskey, a gift from one of his business acquaintances who had owed him a favour and probably still did. It had been a good day. In fact, it had been a wonderful day. He had finally managed to get that old bastard Bart Madison to sign the deal. It hadn't been easy but in the end the old man had seen reason; Edward knew too much and it wouldn't do to have him shooting his mouth off at certain competitors not to mention at Bart's wife.

Edward looked at the first snowflakes floating slowly downward past his windows. He took another generous sip of whiskey and felt the powerful liquor send pleasant warmth coursing through his veins. Yes, life was good, unless of course you started to think about his old man. Why had the old fool chosen a time like this to have a stroke?

Boy, the last couple of days had brought the hell of a need for damage control all right. All those vultures thinking that because his old man was pretty much out of the picture they could move in! Well, Edward "Steady Eddie" Bossiner had showed 'em hadn't he? And by God, he wasn't finished showing them. They'd see that Edward senior had been a pussycat compared to Eddie junior. Still, it was too bad about the old man.

That reminded him, he'd promised his dear mother and his wife Martha, that he'd drop by the hospital to see the old codger. Oh well, promises were made to be broken, right? Anyway, he had better things to do. As for the old lady, he didn't give a hoot what she might think.

Fortunately, he knew he didn't have to worry about Martha; he had trained her well and she was a good wife. She understood their relationship. She gave him his freedom and she didn't ask questions that he wouldn't answer anyway. She was the perfect wife for a businessman of his stature. She kept herself busy with her church and community clubs and her goofy friends.

Maybe it was just as well they hadn't had any kids. He wasn't sure Martha would have been any good at raising them and he sure as hell knew he wouldn't have had the time for it. Kids were nothing but trouble anyway.

I mean, he'd been great for his parents, well for his old man, anyway. He always had been the obedient, agreeable son. When his father had told him to jump, he'd always responded in just the right way. Oh, he'd been smart enough to know that someday all that hypocritical ass-kissing on his part would bear fruit. And of course, he'd been right. People just had to look at him today to know that he was a success, didn't they? Now, mind you, his sister; that was quite another story altogether. Poor Cynthia, she'd never been able to do as she was told. Even as a child, she always had questions. Why this? Why that? God, but she could be an annoying little bitch!

Edward drained the last of the whiskey in the tumbler. The snow was coming down more copiously now. The light flakes were swirling in the gathering wind. There would be another blizzard. Well, he sure didn't care. He had the four by four and this would give him an excuse to get back home late if need be or maybe not at all.

His thoughts drifted back to his sister. He hadn't seen sweet Cynthia since the last disastrous encounter at their parents' place on Labour Day. Why could she never learn to leave well enough alone? Oh no; not dear Cynthia. Always nagging about him and the old man's ways of doing business; complaining that they were ripping off the poor, bitching that some of the apartment buildings they held in the east part of town were a disgrace. Big deal! That foreign scum and low-life should be darn thankful that they even had a roof over their flea-covered heads.

He couldn't believe how different Cynthia was from him. It was too bad really. She could have been such an asset if she'd wanted to follow the old man's advice and gain his business savvy just as he had. Edward didn't much believe that women should be in positions of power, but a guy could make an exception for a sister who showed promise. What a partnership they could have had and still have kept it all in the family! Oh well, her loss. But man, could she bring on a headache. In fact, just thinking about her made him feel like another drink. Well, there was still some time before his appointment, eh? No reason not to have another one. One more for the road as it were; after all, it did look pretty nasty out there.

Edward went to the bar and threw some ice into his glass. From habit, without having to look down at what he was doing, he reached for the decanter and filled the tumbler. He walked over to the windows. It was completely dark now. The snow gave the lights of the city an eerie glow. He could barely make out the surrounding towers through the wind-driven swirls of snow. He could hear the whisper of snowflakes as they whipped the panes of glass inches from his gaze. He felt quite alone really, but at the same time, above it all. As he took a deep swallow of the amber liquid, he felt a surge of power and control. Wow, he could almost feel his heart swell.

For some reason, at that same instant, he felt a momentary nagging thought; he had promised Martha that he would see Doctor Murphy about his blood pressure. Well, that old coot ought to be retired anyhow. It was time to find some new young doctor; one who know what to say, when to say it and whom to say it to. Anyway, who had a half hour to spare for a physical examination at a time like this? He had things to attend to, important things. Yeah, he had to admit it, he was good, and man, he was proud of himself. Hell, why shouldn't he be?

Still, another nagging thought insisted in: Remember your Sunday school lessons, Eddie boy; pride goeth before a fall and all that. Yeah, yeah, but this feels good and I deserve it! He was glad nobody could see him right now; he would have had to pretend that he had been hit hard by his old man's stroke. What a crock!

No, he wasn't about to let something like that ruin his mood tonight. Not even thinking about his bimbo of a sister could do that to him. I mean, can you believe it? Sissy Cynthia's idea of doing something with her life was to become a teacher. What utter crap! A teacher, when she had the chance to work with her old man and her brother! He could still clearly recall the conversation at the table on Labour Day.

"Why won't you go to the Simpsons' party with Douglas?" his mother had asked Cynthia.

"Why? I'll tell you why! Because that arrogant hedonistic bastard thinks he has the world by the balls and he makes me sick, that's why! He's almost as bad as you, Edward!"

"You'll not use language like that in this house! Show some respect to your mother!" had been the old man's classic reply.

"Respect? What's to respect? If you think I respect women or anyone for that matter who do as they're told because they're afraid that showing what they're really made of might upset the way things are, you are really mistaken, dad."

And on and on it had gone throughout that long afternoon. Yeah, Cynthia had been something pissed off that day. Of course, Steady Eddie knew why didn't he? The little chat until two in the morning he'd had with her the night before had left little sister pretty well ready to take his head off. Oh sure, he had been pretty graphic in his descriptions of the way he treated the women who worked for him. What's more, she sure hadn't been impressed with his ideas on handling business and life in general; but what the hell, he had been a little drunk. So what did sweet little sis expect?

Of course he'd never admitted that he was unfaithful to Martha. Stuff like that you kept to yourself as his old man had told him time and time again. That kind of information you did your best to get about other people and you made damn sure they did not know anything like that about you. That kind of knowledge came in handy sooner or later. Didn't **he** know it after today? Still, he had told sis quite a bit and he sometimes regretted it.

Oh what the hell, she'd never dare turn on her own flesh and blood. I mean, she had to know where her bread and butter came from didn't she? Come to think of it though, she had told them all to go to hell that weekend and he hadn't seen her since. That made you kind of wonder how she was getting by didn't it? She had left saying that she'd never set foot in that house again unless there were some major changes, or they were dead. Oh, she was pissed off all right. Ah shit, who needs her? Still, it was too bad. I mean, Douglas Taylor wasn't the only one interested in Cynthia.

There were a lot of pretty big prospects that she could have had with a nod of the head. It could have been really good for the family business. With all that he and his old man knew about these guys, Lord, it could have been one hell of a power boost. Ah, never mind, after today, he knew damn well he could take care of business and he didn't give a flying futon if a few heads had to roll. In fact, he would enjoy it. Some of these old geezer friends of the old man's would find out that Steady Eddie was cut from a slightly more efficient cloth.

Edward was beginning to feel a little light-headed. No point in getting caught driving with an alcohol count over the limit. Getting pulled over by the local guardians of the peace would just complicate the evening, not that it was something that he couldn't take care of. It was time to go anyhow. Time for a little r&r after a hard day's work at the office.

Joe, his trusty underling had set up the appointment with the call girl outfit for seven. It was a little early but the streets wouldn't be great and he had been guaranteed that he would be this little mama's first ever customer. What was her name again? Come on, come on, he'd always prided himself on his ability to remember names. He had to admit that lately though; he wasn't as good at remembering. You know what they say about short term memory when you start pushing forty. No matter, he wasn't stupid and he'd been sure to jot down the address as well as a little hint to remember the babe's name. Ah there it is, oh yeah, Sin-Dee. Oh, wow! With a name like that, how could he go wrong? And it was her first time in business at that! Well, he'd show her a thing or two. He'd give her some opening special. Time to get rolling!

Outside, the wind-driven snow was like a sobering slap in the face of Edward Bossiner. No matter, he felt great and he did need to sober up just a little. He got into the four by four Jeep Grand Cherokee purchased the month before in preparation for the rigours of winter. The whiskey's afterglow filled him with pleasant thoughts, optimism and self-satisfaction. Yes sir, Eddie my man, you sure know just how to plan well ahead to avoid surprises and unpleasantness don't you? He'd sure hate to be driving the Ferrari in this soup.

It took Edward about thirty minutes to get to the penthouse apartment where Joe had set up the appointment. As he had expected, it was quite the setup; most acceptable indeed! Joe knew his tastes and he knew better than to let old Eddy down didn't he?

Edward let himself in with the key provided by Joe. He walked directly to the bedroom. He could see the light under the door of the adjacent bathroom.

"I'm here, sweetheart! Don't bother with the sexy outfit, I don't go for that," he called out.

"I'll be right out," came the answer. Weird, that voice sounded vaguely familiar. Ah, he'd seen so many people in the last two days, it's no wonder voices started to sound the same. He walked over to the window, pushed apart the curtains and looked out at the city. The snow was still coming down. Well, depending on how the next half hour went, he might just have to spend the night. He could think of worse things. After all, Martha would be worried if he were to drive in this storm.

The door of the bathroom opened. Edward turned around. Oh God! No! It couldn't be. It just could **not** be!

"Edward?!?"

"Cynthia...agh...ah...aagghh!?!" Edward gasped as he clutched at his chest and fell face first onto the bed.

Later, the paramedics assured Cynthia that she had done everything possible. She was not to blame herself. Cynthia, however, thought that she would keep to herself how much she had really done. That information was strictly confidential, for herself and for God only.

When Edward Bossiner senior heard of his son's death, it was too much for the old man. He went into shock and did not survive the night.

The funeral was well attended. Expensive limousines lined the driveways of the graveyard. Friends and business associates came to pay their obligatory respect. More than a few were hiding smug feelings of satisfaction behind their mask of sad facial expressions.

The pastor intoned, "Like father, like son. They worked together in life and now in death, they remain side by side."

And indeed, father and son were buried one next to the other in the failing light of a cold and grey December afternoon. More than a few who were gathered there thought that this ending for the two Bossiners was most appropriate and just, but not all thought so for the same reasons.

Later, at the home of the newly-widowed Marlene Bossiner, Cynthia comforted her mother. "It'll be all right, mom. You'll see. You can be yourself now. You won't have to pretend anymore."

"But baby, I've never done anything for myself, not even before I married your father. Someone has always looked after me." She continued with a glazed, far-off look in her eyes, "I have to admit though, I've always been secretly proud of the way you stood up for yourself even as a little girl. You didn't let any of us change you."

"That's all in the past now. We can make things right, mom. We can change a lot of the wrong that's been done. We can do it together you and I," and Cynthia gave her mother that infectious smile so characteristic of her personality as far back as Marlene could remember.

Marlene Bossiner took her daughter's hand, squeezed it gently, and with tears in her eyes, smiled back.

LE LOUP BLANC

Il était une fois loin dans les bois inconnus des hommes d'aujourd'hui, une vieille femme qui vivait dans une petite chaumière avec un chat et une chouette. Cette femme avait vécu dans cette région toute sa vie; la plupart du temps seule. Lorsqu'elle voulait se l'admettre, elle ne savait vraiment même plus combien d'étés elle avait vus. Elle savait simplement qu'elle était vieille, très vieille. Elle ne se rappelait plus combien de chats ni de chouettes avaient demeurés avec elle, passant leur vie à l'écouter murmurer; à la regarder faire ses affaires de vieille femme, car il leur semblait qu'elle avait toujours été vieille.

Au temps où se passe cette histoire, l'hiver était descendu sur la région depuis plusieurs jours. Les arbres étaient recouverts d'une épaisse couche de neige. Ceci les faisait ressembler à des fantômes lorsque la lune se montrait durant les longues nuits glaciales. Les animaux des environs étaient, soit couchés pour l'hiver, soit à essayer de se trouver quelque chose à manger et à ne pas geler.

Un de ces animaux s'appelait Lobo. C'était un magnifique loup tout à fait blanc qui semblait disparaître complètement de temps en temps dès que la neige avait recouvert le sol. Bien souvent, la nuit, on ne voyait que ses deux yeux verts qui brillaient dans la noirceur comme deux étoiles jumelles égarées.

Au temps duquel nous parlons, un changement énorme était en train d'essayer de s'établir dans cette région particulière de la forêt paisible. Des hommes venus de quelque pays lointain avaient réussi à découvrir cet endroit et il y avait un grand danger qu'ils allaient changer la demeure des animaux, de Lobo, de la vieille femme et de son chat et de sa chouette pour toujours.

Ces hommes n'étaient pas bienfaisants. Ils se réjouissaient à détruire, à tuer, et à changer à permanence les lieux dans lesquels ils pénétraient; même s'ils ne s'en rendaient pas compte.

On devait faire quelque chose. Les animaux ainsi que la vieille femme en étaient persuadés. Mais, que faire? Les méchants envahisseurs avaient des armes à feu et ils ne semblaient pas avoir de conscience. On les entendait tard dans la nuit. Ils chantaient, ils criaient; et il était bien évident qu'ils s'enivraient tous les soirs. Quelquefois, après une de ces nuits particulièrement bruyante, les animaux de la forêt trouvaient deux ou trois de ces êtres maléfiques endormis au milieu du jour. Rien n'aurait été plus facile que de les supprimer sur place, mais le code de la forêt ne leur permettait pas d'agir ainsi. Donc, le danger continuait.

Le printemps approchait. On sentait une certaine douceur parfumée dans l'air. Les arbres qui dormaient depuis plusieurs mois commençaient à s'éveiller sous leur épaisse écorce brune et rugueuse. Mais il fallait tout de même vraiment connaître les façons de la nature et de la terre de cette région pour sentir que la saison de renouveau n'était plus très loin, car les nuits étaient toujours froides et un givre épais qui donnait un aspect féerique aux arbres les recouvrait chaque matin.

Dans un endroit un peu éloigné du camp des hommes, la vieille femme devenait de plus en plus inquiète. Elle se rendait compte que les nouveaux venus s'avançaient chaque jour de davantage près de sa demeure. Elle savait bien qu'ils finiraient par découvrir son paisible logis. Durant sa longue existence, elle avait rencontré bien des obstacles, et chaque fois elle les avait surmontés; mais elle n'avait jamais eu à faire face à de tels êtres; des hommes armés. En effet, comme nous l'avons lu plus tôt, ces nouveaux envahisseurs semblaient complètement sans conscience. Ils répandaient le mal par ci et par là sans se soucier de la destruction et du mal qu'ils faisaient aux habitants de la forêt. Il fallait faire quelque chose sans plus tarder et la vieille femme prit une décision. Elle allait parler à Lobo. Ce protecteur de la forêt lui viendrait en aide; elle en était persuadée.

Donc, par une nuit de pleine lune, elle sortit de chez elle pour faire rendez-vous avec le loup mystérieux. Elle savait où il aimait se promener lorsque la lune voyageait dans le ciel et elle le trouva sans difficulté. Elle se mit à lui parler, à lui expliquer la situation fâcheuse dans laquelle se trouvait la forêt. Quoique Lobo ne puisse pas lui répondre, elle voyait bien qu'il comprenait et elle rentra chez elle convaincue que Lobo ferait ce qu'il se devait de faire.

Le lendemain soir, on pouvait remarquer un cercle qui entourait l'astre couchant qui dominait le ciel. En effet, la lune aussi semblait différente; un peu plus pâle que la nuit précédente. Quoique les animaux de la forêt ainsi que la vieille femme avaient pu s'en rendre compte; les hommes, étant nouveaux venus dans la région, ne comprirent pas ce que signifiaient ni le cercle autour du soleil couchant ni la pâleur de la lune. Comme d'habitude, ils commencèrent à boire, à rire, à raconter des histoires plus ou moins croyables, et éventuellement ils tombèrent dans un lourd sommeil.

Vers le milieu de la nuit, le vent commença à souffler. Les arbres se mirent à gémir et la neige descendit sur la forêt. Peu à peu, les hommes du camp s'éveillèrent. Ils avaient beaucoup de difficulté à se rendre compte de ce qui se passait. Le temps qui avait semblé s'approcher du printemps avait soudainement fait demi tour vers le nord, vers le froid, et vers l'hiver. Les hommes grelottaient dans leurs tentes. Le vent devenait de plus en plus fort. Des branches mortes tombaient des arbres et peu à peu, les tentes furent percées par ces objectifs. Les hommes commençaient à avoir peur. Ce changement si soudain de la température ne leur semblait pas normal. Quelque chose n'allait pas. Tout à coup, ils crurent entendre un hurlement affreux. Était-ce le vent; un arbre abattu peut-être? Les hommes étaient maintenant effrayés. Ils ne pouvaient plus rester dans leurs tentes qui commençaient à s'écraser ou à s'envoler dans la tempête. Donc, ils se décidèrent de sortir. À peine dehors, ils entendirent encore une fois le hurlement affreux. Ils tournèrent les yeux dans la direction dont venait le cri redoutable et, en ce moment, entre une bourrasque de vent, ils purent voir le magnifique loup blanc. Les hommes furent immédiatement pris d'une terreur indescriptible. Ils restèrent quelques instants figés sur place, incapables de bouger. Puis, lorsque les hurlements de Lobo cessèrent, ils se mirent à courir à travers la forêt dans la direction par laquelle ils étaient venus. Ils ne prirent même pas le temps d'apporter leurs effets avec eux. Ils firent leur chemin aussi vite que possible vers les régions desquelles ils étaient venus. Quelques uns d'entre eux ne furent pas capables de survivre la tempête. Ceux-ci finirent par perdre leurs forces et tombèrent dans la neige, endormis pour toujours. Quoiqu'il en soit, au moins un de ces mauvais hommes se retrouva parmi les régions "civilisées" car cette légende a pu être passée de génération en génération jusqu'aujourd'hui puisque nous avons la possibilité de la connaître.

On ne sait pas ce qui est devenu de la vieille femme, de sa chouette, de son chat, des animaux de la forêt, et de Lobo dont nous venons d'entendre l'histoire; mais il est fort probable qu'ils sont toujours ensemble dans cette merveilleuse forêt qui demeure inconnue des hommes de notre ère. Et, mes amis, si elle réussit à demeurer inconnue, il y a bien des chances que d'autres légendes en sortiront.

... *Bonne nuit et dormez bien, petits enfants de la Terre.*

TOADFACE

(some adult language)

It was a Friday night. Todd and his best friend Mike were hanging out, just looking for something to happen. Todd was driving his mother's car, a 1990 Honda Civic. He remembered when his father had surprised her with it. It was her birthday and his dad had come home from work at the usual time. He hadn't even wished her a happy birthday that day but that made it obvious that he'd not forgotten. Todd's father was not very good at hiding his feelings and it had been quite evident that he'd been up to something. He'd been planning for this for some time. Todd knew that his mom and dad didn't have a lot of money. He also knew that they were happy. And, he knew they loved him...

...But all of that was before his dad had suddenly packed up and left. That day had remained painfully fresh in his memory. His father had come home visibly upset. He and his mom had gone into their bedroom and Todd could hear them talking in low voices. Although he could not hear what was being said, it was obvious that something was seriously wrong. Shortly afterwards, his dad had come out with a back pack, he'd hugged him, kissed his wife and left. It was dark by then and he had not taken the car. It was impossible to see in which direction he had gone. Not that it would have mattered. The town was surrounded by miles of hilly, heavily wooded terrain where anyone with a reasonable knowledge of the woods could probably manage quite well and perhaps vanish if they so wished. Todd knew that there were several abandoned trappers' cabins scattered about throughout the forest. But for all that he knew, his dad might as well have hopped on a freight train to Canada. That night was the last Todd had seen of him and it was hard to believe that over six months had already gone by.

At first, his mother would say nothing of the reason for his father's decision to leave. As the weeks went by however, she finally relented to Todd's constant demands to tell him the truth. She began to let Todd in on some of the details. Little by little, he was able to piece these together to finally understand what had happened.

There had been some argument at his father's workplace. Milt Harley, a cantankerous, evil-tempered man at the best of times had ended up with a six-inch spike through the middle of his forehead. It was not difficult to figure out that an air hammer had done the damage, however, when the sheriff began to ask questions as to who might have been holding the hammer at the time, things became rather murkier.

To make a long story short, Todd's father became the culprit when several other employees came forward the next day and accused him of having provoked Harley into an argument and "nailing" him in the head (if you would please pardon the pun, sheriff). His mother told Todd that his father had been sure that someone had threatened his co-workers.

The Harley family was known to exert quite a lot of influence in town and it was well-known that the sheriff, who was married to a cousin of Harley's, would often turn a blind eye to the family's less than honest dishing out of their own brand of justice. Todd's father had not waited for the sheriff to show up with a warrant. He had clearly felt that he did not stand a chance against such small-town conspiratorial odds. Todd was assured by his mother that the nail had not come from his father's air hammer and Todd, knowing his father's gentle disposition, believed her.

Now, as Todd drove through the almost-deserted streets of the town on this grey December dusk, he thought again of his father. He had been thinking a lot about him of late and, every time that he did, he felt anger rise from within the deep reaches of his soul.

"Give me a beer, Mike," he said.

"Hey, man, you're driving," Mike retorted.

"So what? You think I'm gonna be impaired on one shitty light beer? Give me a break, man. Pass it over."

Mike reluctantly took a can out of the case on the floor by his feet. He looked ahead at the first lazy snowflakes drifting in front of the headlights. All day the weather office had been promising the first heavy storm of the season and as the darkness deepened, it definitely seemed as though the weather people had been right in their prognosis. He said, "Hey, Todd, it's going to snow. We should go home before the roads get bad. Your mom said we should be back by supper anyway. You don't want her taking the car from you for a couple of weeks do you?"

"Fuck you, Mike," Todd answered angrily. "You know, you're getting to be a real pain in the ass lately. Mr. Wonderful Son and Mr. Super Student and whatever else. I'm getting sick and fed up with my mom constantly reminding me of what a great guy you are. If you got a problem with my driving, why don't you just get out right now?"

"Take it easy, Todd. I didn't mean anything about your driving. It's just that I like your mom. She's a really nice person, you know. I don't want to cause her any hassles; that's all. Man, you've been really tense lately. You know how sorry everybody is about your dad. I wish I could do something about it, you know we all do. You've got to chill out, man."

"Chill out. Yeah, sure. Easy for you to say. It's not your old man that's just up and left you is it? Oh, forget it, you wouldn't understand anyway." Todd took another sip of his beer. He looked ahead at the multitude of snowflakes rushing towards the headlights. Then, without warning, he put on the brakes. "Hey, Mike, look! It's Toadface!"

Mike looked out the side window. Sure enough, there he was, the Toadman. This individual had started coming into town once a week for about six months now. He never spoke to anyone. He always wore heavy clothing and a large, wide-brimmed hat. It was hard to make out his face but those who had managed a fairly close look at what little they could see of it swore that he looked like a toad. Nothing was known about him except that he obviously lived in the woods.

"Hey, Mike, I'm gonna give Toadface a bit of scare. Watch this!"

"Hold it, Todd! Take it easy, man. What are you doing? Leave the guy alone. Come on, let's go home. It's snowing too much anyway."

"Fuck off, Mike! I'm just gonna spray a little snow in his face. That psycho deserves it. I swear, man, he's been staring at our house once too many times for my comfort. He just stops and sits there and stares for a minute or two. He's creepy I tell you."

Todd stepped on the accelerator. The car swerved towards the sidewalk spraying snow high in the air.

Todd rolled down his window. He screamed, "Hey, Toadface! How do you like this you chicken shit psycho? Whooeee, Mikey! This is fun!" With mounting dread, Mike watched as the Honda skidded towards the helpless Toadface. The latter looked up in horror a split second before the impact threw him like a test dummy into the air and the falling snow.

Todd screamed, "Oh, God! No! I didn't mean to! Oh, shit! Look! Mike! His face came off! I saw his face come off! Oh God! I must be drunk! Please let this not be real!"

As the car came to a stop, Mike ran out to the inert figure on the sidewalk. There in the snow, next to the man lying in the growing pool of blood by his head was a cheap

Halloween mask. He bent down to look. His heart froze.   "Oh my dear God!" he cried. He was looking into the dying eyes of Todd's father.

TI GUS AN' M'SIEUR L'DIABLE

Hé mes amis! My friends! I am reddy to tell de storee now. But you know, dis storee is ver' old an you might not b'lieve it. But hit is all true. It 'appen wen my arriére grand-pére, how you say, ...uh..., backward gran'fadder, well 'e was jus' a young man. 'E tell de storee to my gran'fadder an' my gran'fadder 'e tell it to my fadder an' my fadder tell it to me; an' now, mes amis, I tell hit to you, hein?

It 'appen in de village of Saint 'Poléon. Now I know dere are doze of you dere who will say dat dere was never dat village. Well, I tell you dere was a place call by dat name right 'ere before de big cité swallow hit up. Saint 'Poléon was ver' cloze to de river. Anoway, de storee she all start one night at de veillée. De veillée dat is wen everybody get together for talking and singing and dancing and mebbee some drinking too. You guys call dat a partee. Well anoway, dis veillée was at de 'ouse of de bonhomme Gauthier dat night an' everybody was dere talking an' laughing an' mebbee drinking, an' hafter some tam, l'bonhomme Gauthier, 'e pick up 'is violon an' 'e begin to play. Not long hafter, Jacques Leduc e' take 'is accordéon an' den odders dey take dere 'armonica an' de spoon an' before you know hit, everybody is dancing except de curé who jus' look. Dis is wen Ti Gus come in from houtside all cover wid snow. Well, I 'ave to tell you habout Ti Gus. 'E was de strongest an' de mos' 'ansome young man in Saint 'Poléon, an' all de girls, dey want to dance wit 'im an' mebbe dey tink 'e might decide to take one of dem for a wife. But Ti Gus, 'e never seem to care much about hany girl in particulier. 'E dance wid de skinny one an' wid de fat one jus' de same. 'E dance wid de short one an' 'e dance wid de tall one. 'E dance wid de pretty one an' wid de ugly one. 'E dance wid de young one an' wid de old one. 'E not seem to mand any girl at all. So de odder young man dey don' mand Ti Gus an' 'e is popular wid everyone in de village.

So dis veillée she is going pretty good. Dere is dancing an' laughing an' of course, dere is a li'l bit of drinking too hein? Jus' for a li'l fun on Saturday night at de 'house of de bonhomme Gauthier. So everybody is 'aving good tam an' hit is quite noisy wen soudainement, dere is de knock on de door. Ol' man Gauthier 'e yell out, "Come in, come in!" De door she open an' everybody stop an' look because dere at de door is le diable, ...uh..., how you guys say dat, ...uh..., oh yes, de devil. An' 'e 'as wit him a beautiful young lady.

Nobody ever seen 'er before but everybody know le diable. 'E look like a 'ansome guy except for de big tail sticking out de back an' de two 'orn on 'is 'ead.

Well, de devil 'e say, "Bonsoir tout le monde. I 'ear all dat noise an' de musique an' I feel like a li'l whiskey so 'ere I am. Hi 'ope you don' mand I put my 'orse in de barn. I didn' come in because I'm cold even dough dere is de paradis of a tempête out dere." Paradis, dat mean 'eaven; an' tempête, ...humm..., dat is wat you say is a blizzard in de winter. Anoway, 'e laugh wen 'e say dat. HA! HA! HA! But nobody laugh. Den 'e say, "Dis is Lisette Lemaire from de village of Chutes Vertes." Now dat is why nobody know dis girl because Chutes Vertes is far up de river from Saint 'Poléon. Anoway, de devil e' spot de curé an' den 'e say, "Hé, curé, I know a few li'l ting dat I could tell but I will say notting if you keep houtta my way." An' de curé 'e turn red like a big fat cherree an' 'e say notting at all, jus' sit dere an' 'e look very hembarrassed. So den de devil say, "Mebbe Lisette want to dance. She might not get de chance again to dance at de veillée like dis." An' again 'e laugh. HA! HA! HA! An' den 'e go an' get some whiskey an' e' sit down ver' ver' cloze to de fire even dough 'e say 'e was not cold. Mebbe de fire remin' 'im of 'is 'ouse. I don' know.

Anoway, now Ti Gus 'e come over an' begin to talk wid de belle Lisette. She look so beautiful but so sad. Dey dance but my arriére grand-pére, dat is my backward grand-fadder for you guys, 'e see dat dey are mos'ly talking. An' so Ti Gus find out dat Lisette fadder 'as ver' big problème. 'E lak to play wid de money, ...uh..., 'ow you say dat, ...uh, ... ah oui, 'e lak to gamble. An' wat 'ad 'appen is dat Lisette fadder 'ad play wid de devil an' e' lose. So 'e 'ad to give Lisette to de devil or de devil will 'ave take de 'ole fam'ly.

Well, now Ti Gus 'e tinks an' tinks. An' den, 'e get an idee. 'E go to de devil an' 'e say, "Hé, M'sieur I'diable, I 'av somting to propose to you." Now everybody know dat de devil 'e his always ready to make de bargain because 'e tinks 'e can always win. So de devil say, "Vas-y, Ti Gus, go ahead, tell me wat you propose." An' Ti Gus say dis. "Let's have de contest to see which one of us is better for cutting de trees. If you win de contest, you can 'ave me but if I win, den Lisette she is free to go." Now, de devil 'e laugh again. HA! HA! HA! An' den 'e say, "Don' you know I ham de best bûcheron dat can be foun' anywhere?" For doze of you don' know, de bûcheron 'e is de lumberjack. But anoway, de devil e' continue an' 'e say to Ti Gus, "If you want to try, allons-y, let's go tomorrow morning at seven-tirty." But Ti Gus 'e say, "Not tomorrow, hit tis de Sunday." An, dats wen de curé 'e make a li'l noise in 'is troat, lak a frog but 'e say notting. Now, I guess de devil is in a good 'umour hafter de whiskey because 'e say wid a big smile, "C'est bon, all right, let's do it on Monday morning."

Hafter dat, de veillée stop because everyone is tinking too much about Ti Gus an' de devil an' de poor Lisette. So everybody go home to bed an' de next morning, de church is more full dan even at Chrissmass for de messe de minuit, dat is de mass of midnight. Dat Sunday, everyting is pretty quiet in de village. Dere's not much laughing or talking at de table an' everybody go to bed early dat night hafter de rosary.

Well, Monday come an' de men 'ave measure two equal parties in de woods for de contest. It is col' but de sun 'e will be shining dat day an' it seem lak a good day of de winter. At seven-tirty exactement, de devil arrive wid 'is haxe. Ti Gus is already dere waiting. As soon as de signal is give, de devil begin to cut. 'E is ver' good an' fast an' de trees dey fall dis way an' dat way. But Ti Gus 'e is ver' good too. Wid ev'ry swing of 'is haxe, two or tree trees fall dis way an' dat way lak de weeds. Hafter some tam, Ti Gus 'e get tirsty so 'e go down to de river for some wadder. But as soon as 'e turn 'is back, de devil take de haxe of Ti Gus an' trow it far over de 'ill. Ti Gus come back an' e say notting. 'E jus' go an' get anoder haxe dat 'e 'ad bring an' 'ide under de snow jus' near dat place where dey work. De devil 'e don' look ver' 'appy an' 'e go down for some wadder too. Den dey continue to cut an' de trees fall dis way an' dat way an' some even go flying up into de blue sky lak straw in de wind in de summer wen we do de battage. For doze of you don' know, de battage is de trashing of de crop. Anoway, de next tam Ti Gus go for some wadder, de devil come beeind 'im 'an 'e give Ti Gus a big kick wid 'is big boot an' Ti Gus 'e go flying into de middle of de river. De devil 'e laugh an' laugh. HA! HA! HA! HA! HA! Well, Ti Gus 'e jus' come out an' shake de wadder from 'is cloze an' 'e go back to de work. But dis tam hafter a few minute, 'e 'say somting to de devil. 'E say dis, "Eh, M'sieur l'diable," (dat mean Mister Devil for dose of you din' unnerstan'); Ti Gus say, "Tanks for de cooling off. I needed dat! An' dis tam, Ti Gus laugh. HA! HA! HA! 'E laugh because 'e know de devil don' lak it cool.

Dey go back to work again but now doze who watch see dat de devil is getting mad. Dey can see de smoke come hout of 'is ear an' hout of 'is nose an' mebbe hout of somewhere else too but dey don' say hit because hit tis not proper, but dey know hit tis de smoke an' not de vapeur because de smoke, she is black.

Ti Gus an' de devil, dey keep on but now de devil is hangry an' 'e work ver' ver' fas'. But Ti Gus 'e work ver' ver' fas' also. De devil is surprise dat Ti Gus can almos' keep up to 'im. So de next tam Ti Gus goes for wadder, de devil get really bad an' 'e trow 'is haxe at de back of Ti Gus to try to kill 'im. But someone yell 'an Ti Gus, 'e jus' turn 'haroun quick an' 'e jus' take de haxe hout of de air an' 'give hit back to de devil. Dis tam, Ti Gus look very serious an' 'e say to de devil, "It look to me lak you 'ave different rule wen you 'ave de contest, M'sieur l'diable." An' 'e jus' go back to cut more trees.

Now doze watching see dat de devil is really hangry. 'E cut faster an' faster an' dere is smoke coming from all over 'im. Hafter some tam I guess 'e get tirsty because 'e go down to de river for wadder. But dis tam, as soon as 'e bend down to have some wadder, Ti Gus run quick an' quiet an' 'e poigne la queue du diable, oh, excuse me, 'e grab de tail of de devil an' 'e quick tie hit to one of de trees dat is dere. Well, now de devil is furieux, ver' ver' hangry an' ver' mad. 'E yell an' e' swear terrible an' de black smoke she is all hover 'is bodee. But Ti Gus 'e jus' go on cutting de trees until 'e is finish.

Now, I know some of you won' b'lieve dis but de devil wen 'e see dat Ti Gus win, 'e start to cry an' 'e beg Ti Gus to let 'im go. Well Ti Gus, 'e is a fair guy an' 'e let de devil go. Well, de devil 'e say notting. 'E jus' run true de trees an' soon everybody see 'im go by lak de wind on 'is black 'orse an' dey don' see 'im hagain.

Now Ti Gus go back to tell Lisette an' she send a message to 'er fam'ly an' later dey 'ear dat 'er fadder is so tankful dat 'e stop de gambling an' de playing wid de money an' de cards.

Anoway, dat night dere is a spéciale veillée, dis tam at de 'ouse of de bonhomme Boulé. Everybody is 'appy an' slap Ti Gus on de back. But dere 'as been a change in Ti Gus. Wen de dancing begin, 'e only dance wit' Lisette. An' wen de musiciens take a pause, 'e only talk wit' Lisette. An' doze who were dere dey say dat 'e 'ad a diff'rent look in 'is eye. Now de odder girl dey were désappointées but dey were also 'appy for Ti Gus an' for poor Lisette who 'ad such a bad scare by de devil.

Anoway, not long hafter dat, dere was a marriage an' dat wedding was de best dat everybody 'ad ever see in Saint 'Poléon. An' de way dat belle Lisette look, everybody know dat soon, dere might be a li'l Ti Gus or a li'l Lisette come along.

Well, mes amis, dat is my storee about Ti Gus an' de devil. Dere are many odder storee habout Ti Gus but dat is for some odder tam, hein? Tabarnouche! Look at de clock! Hit his nine-tirty. It his my tam for de bed. Bonsoir, my friends. So long for now mes amis. Remember to say your prayer. Aroun' 'ere, we know dat de devil don' forget even dough 'e tink **we** might forget.

HOW TI' GUS GOT 'IS FIRS' DOG

Hé les amis, venez! Come, my friends! I am reddy to tell dis udder storree about Ti' Gus now. Dis one is habout 'ow 'e get 'is firs' dog. Hit 'appen when Ti' Gus was living in de village of Saint Hercule. I 'av tell mannee storrees about Ti' Gus and dis one is ver' old too an when I tell a storee habout Ti' Gus I always say dat you might not b'lieve hit. But like all de odder storree, hit is all true. It 'appen wen my arriére grand-pére, how you say, ...uh..., my backward gran'fadder was jus' a young guy. 'E tell de storree to my gran'fadder an' my gran'fadder 'e tell hit to my fadder an' my fadder tell hit to me; an' now, mes amis, I tell hit to you, hein?

Dis is 'ow de storee 'appen. Hit twas late in de sommer an' hit was de tam to do de moisson, dat is when we bring in de crop, you say de 'arvest I think. On dat day, Ti' Gus was working on de farm of 'is oncle, le bonhomme Thibault. De day was hot, de sky was blue and de sun was shining. Ti' Gus 'ad take 'is shirt off 'an 'is bodee was brown and 'is muscles dey were shining from de sweating. 'Is job was to trow de gerbes d'avoine, what you guys call de bunches of oat, to de guys on de wagon. Ti' Gus 'e work so fass dat dey 'ad to tell 'im to slow down all de tam. Ever'ting was going jus' fan until soudainement, a ver' big bear come hout of de woods by de field. De bear was ver' ver' big and ver' ver' hangree and mebbee e' was hongree too. De 'orses get scare and dey run off wid de wagon in de odder direction follow by all de guys who work. But not Ti' Gus. Ti' Gus, 'e jus' turn haround to face de bear 'an 'e start to run to de bear and 'e yell and yell. De bear, 'e was so surprise dat 'e stop and sit down on 'is big behin'. 'E look lak mebbee 'e was tinking, "Dis is one crazee guy." But Ti' Gus come to de bear and 'e say dis,

> You big bad bear,
>
> what you doing dere?
>
> You 'av no right
>
> to start dis fight.
>
> Dis not de place
>
> to show your face.
>
> We 'av work to do
>
> so scoobeedoo..."

or someting lak dat. Hi don' remember ever'ting. But Ti' Gus was always good wid de words 'an one tam 'e win a contest at de school and de bonne soeur, dat is de nonn, she gave 'im a prize. But dat 'is hanodder storree for some odder day, hein?

Anoway, hafter a few minute, de bear 'e start to get hangree again 'an 'e start to come for Ti' Gus. Well, mes amis, dat was de biggess mistake 'e could do. Ti' Gus jump up in de air and 'e 'op on de back of de bear. De bear is furieux den and 'e grunt and groan and growl and shake but Ti' Gus, 'e 'ang on. Dis go on for some tam. Doze dat 'ad run away, dey start coming back when dey see dat Ti' Gus is riding de bear lak de cowboy ride de 'orse at de rodeo at de Calgaree stompede. Pretty soon, de bear get tired an' 'e stop jumping up and down an' finalement, 'e jus' lie down an' moan lak 'e mebbee crying.

Well, Ti' Gus, 'e waste no tam. 'E ask for de bridle from de 'orses which somebodee 'ad bring back. 'E take de bridle and 'e tie hit haround de neck of de bear. Den, 'e tie de bear to a tree dat was not far from dere an' everybodee go back to work.

Hafter de crop is all on de wagon, Ti' Gus come for de bear. 'E say ver' loud and ver' strong,

> "Hé, Monsieur bear,
> you 'ear me clair.
> When I set you free
> from dis dere tree,
> you better be good

an' go back to your wood..."

or someting lak dat. I tink hit twas more long. But, has you can see, dat Ti' Gus, 'e was a vrai poète.

Well, to de surprise of everyone, wen Ti' Gus untie de bear, de bear jus' stay dere and look at Ti' Gus. And wen Ti' Gus walk away, de bear start to follow 'im an' 'e follow 'im all de way back to de village.

Dat was 'ow Ti' Gus come to 'ave a dog even dough hit was really a bear. Ti' Gus call 'im Nounours which mean teddy bear in henglish.

Nounours was a ver' ver' good chien de garde, dat mean a dog of guard; an' Ti' Gus din' 'av to worree habout losing any more chicken to de wolve or de raccoon. Halso, from den on de people always hask 'im permission before dey borrow tings and dey always remember to bring dem back aldough dey prefer dat Nounours was tie up before dey come to visit.

De storree say dat Ti' Gus and Nounours, dey 'ad a 'appy life but dat was before Ti' Gus fall in love and get marry.

And dat, mes amis is hanoder storree for hanoder day too.

ANIMAUX TACITURNES

J'ai voulu parler à ceux qui habitent dans la forêt.
Je m'y suis dirigé de bon matin.

Sur l'étang calme, un canard nageait paisiblement.
Quand il m'a vu, il s'est enfui affolé.

J'ai espéré parler à l'écureuil nerveux,
Mais dès qu'il m'a aperçu, il s'est caché.

Déçu, j'ai appelé le geai bavard
Mais il m'a évité sans m'avoir parlé.

Au bord d'un ruisseau calme, le héron bleu pêchait;
Mais comme je voulais l'adresser
Il s'est envolé sans rien dire.

À la lisière d'une clairière, un lapin brun mangeait.
Je me suis approché de lui, mais il a disparu.

Une fauvette chantait, j'en suis sûr;

Je me suis approché d'elle;

Aussitôt qu'elle m'a vu, elle aussi s'est envolée.

Un gros raton laveur masqué venait vers moi.

Je l'ai appelé; il a fait demi tour et je ne l'ai plus vu.

Une jolie petite perdrix cherchait dans les feuilles mortes.

J'ai voulu l'observer mais elle n'est pas restée.

Un ours lourd passait non loin de moi;

Il m'a lancé un coup d'oeil, il a grogné, et il s'est éloigné.

Un serpent et une araignée jasaient tout près.

J'ai voulu me joindre à eux mais en me voyant, ils se sont quittés.

Du haut d'un sapin vert, un aigle majestueux observait la forêt.

J'ai pensé lui parler; il m'a regardé d'un oeil froid et il s'en est allé.

Un doux chevreuil cherchait un pré où il aurait pu manger.

Dès qu'il m'a vu, il s'est élancé dans l'autre direction.

Un papillon tardif s'attardait sur une fleur.
J'allais le saluer quand il s'est envolé.

Enfin j'ai rencontré un petit escargot qui s'en allait lentement.
Il ne pouvait pas s'échapper et je lui ai demandé ce qui s'était
passé.

Il m'a répondu que demain
Ça serait la saison de la chasse.

C'est alors que j'ai tout compris.
Tristement, je suis rentré chez moi.

KIPPER, THE COW

Once there was a cow that lived with her family and friends in a meadow. The meadow was in a valley high up in the mountains. The cow's name was Kipper. Kipper loved the meadow because the grass was always fresh, green, and plentiful. Through the meadow there flowed a stream. When Kipper went to drink from the cool mountain water, she often saw the fish that lived in the stream. Kipper loved to talk with the fish because they always had interesting stories to tell.

The fish were salmon that traveled far away to the sea and back again. On their journey, they saw a great many things, some wonderful and some terrible. Kipper was only interested in the wonderful things. She did not want to hear about the terrible things and she quickly forgot about them. Every time that Kipper spoke with the fish, she wished that she could leave the meadow and go on a long journey as well.

One day, a strong and very cold wind blew a storm over the mountains and into the valley where Kipper and the others were grazing in the meadow. The sky grew dark and snow began to fall. It snowed and snowed and snowed. Soon, everything was covered with a thick blanket and the cows could not find the grass. Kipper, her family, and friends became very hungry. They had to leave the meadow and go down the mountain to find food.

As the journey went on, Kipper was happy. At last, she had a chance to see the world outside the valley where she had always lived.

After several days of travel, the herd came to a large valley where there were many other cows. The grass was fresh and lush and the hungry cows ate until they were satisfied.

Everything went well until one day Kipper heard the sound of horses galloping and men shouting. In a moment, all was confusion. Her family and friends began to run in a panic. A great cloud of dust rose in the air. The cowboys shouted and waved their arms as they rounded up the cows. In the excitement and panic, Kipper found herself separated from the others, and, unseen by the cattlemen, she hid among some large rocks.

Soon, all was quiet in the valley. Kipper came out of her hiding place to find the prairie empty and desolate; she felt alone and filled with sadness.

Not long afterwards, Kipper decided to return to her meadow in the mountains. As she journeyed through the forest, she came upon another of her kind. Like herself, he had been separated from his family in the confusion of the stampede in the valley. His name was Ramón. Kipper told him about the place where she had come from. Soon, Ramón and Kipper were back in the lovely meadow away high in the mountains.

Kipper and Ramón were happy in the meadow. Not long afterwards, they had a baby. They named him, Steadfast. Many more followed and after some years, the meadow once again was home to a large extended family of cows.

Kipper still spoke to the fish in the stream and she enjoyed their stories but, as she raised her children, she taught them to be happy where they were. As she told them the story of the storm and all that came of it, she also emphasized that the grass is not always greener on the other side of the fence. (Oh, I know, that is corny… …but see me smile.)

CHENI

Cheni est une toute petite créature. Elle vient de naître hier et à vrai dire; elle n'est pas beaucoup plus grosse qu'un grain de riz. Si elle en avait la capacité, elle pourrait danser le rock 'n roll sur l'ongle du plus petit doigt de votre main. Savez-vous de quel d'animal je vous parle? Non? Pas encore? Eh bien, je vais vous donner encore quelques détails:

Elle a de petites pattes presque invisibles, ce qui veut dire qu'on a de la peine à les voir. Vous ne savez pas encore de quel animal je veux vous parler? Bon, alors, voici encore quelques indices: Celle dont je vous raconte l'histoire de sa journée est de couleur verte mais elle a des cousins et des cousines qui sont de couleurs différentes. Elle aime ronger les feuilles des arbres. De plus, si elle a la chance, elle aime quelquefois se faire une maison dans une pomme. Ah, vous avez deviné de quoi (ou de qui) il s'agit. Mais oui, bien sûr; Cheni est une chenille.

Ce matin, le soleil réveille Cheni de bonne heure. Les couleurs du ciel annoncent une journée d'été magnifique. Quelques nuages flottent dans le ciel de l'aurore. Ils sont bleus, roses, oranges, et violets. Les rayons du soleil levant caressent les feuilles du pommier dans lequel Cheni habite et réchauffent son petit corps vert.

Cheni a faim. Elle commence à chercher une feuille tendre et pleine de jus. Elle s'avance le long des branches en examinant les feuilles qu'elle rencontre. Avant longtemps, elle en trouve une qui lui semble particulièrement appétissante. Elle commence à manger. Plus elle ronge, moins elle a faim.

Bientôt, ayant fini son déjeuner, elle regarde par le trou qu'elle vient de faire dans la feuille. Elle imagine que c'est une fenêtre par laquelle elle peut voir un nouveau monde. Tout à coup, en regardant par sa fenêtre, elle aperçoit Abi, une abeille du voisinage. Abi semble-t-il à Cheni, travaille toujours. Ce matin, comme d'habitude, elle passe à la recherche de fleurs d'été qui poussent dans le verger de pommiers.

"Coucou!" s'écrie Cheni. "Viens jouer à cache-cache, Abi!"

"Je ne peux pas, Cheni. Je dois trouver des fleurs. L'hiver s'approche et nous devons mettre de côté assez à manger avant son arrivée."

"L'hiver?" répond Cheni. "Mais, qu'est-ce que c'est?"

"Tu verras quand tu seras plus grande," lui dit Abi.

"Pourquoi dois-tu trouver des fleurs?" demande Cheni.

"Mais pour faire du miel, bien sûr," réplique Abi.

"Qu'est-ce que vous faites avec ce miel?" insiste Cheni.

"Nous le mangeons. Et maintenant je dois partir; j'ai beaucoup à faire avant le coucher du soleil. À bientôt, Cheni."

"Bon, d'accord; au revoir, Abi." lui répond Cheni.

Cheni est un peu déçue, mais elle a peu de temps à y réfléchir car tout à coup, elle entend un grand bourdonnement. Elle se demande ce que cela peut bien être. Elle a même un peu peur. Mais quelques instants plus tard, elle se rend compte que tout ce bruit est fait par un autre habitant du verger. C'est Bouzi, le bourdon, qui lui aussi cherche les fleurs estivales.

"Salut, Bouzi;" lui crie Cheni. "Où vas-tu? As-tu le temps de jouer à cache-cache avec moi?"

"Bonjour, Cheni!" lui dit Bouzi. "Je regrette, mais je n'ai pas le temps de jouer avec toi aujourd'hui. Il fait beau et je dois chercher des fleurs pour faire du miel."

"Toi aussi?" demande Cheni.

"Mais oui, ma petite. Il me faut profiter du beau temps. L'hiver n'est pas aussi loin qu'il le semble. À plus tard."

Cheni décide de se promener par les branches du pommier. Elle n'a fait que quelques pas de chenille quand elle rencontre Frémi, une des nombreuses fourmis qui habitent dans les environs.

"Hé, Frémi!" crie Cheni. "Veux-tu jouer avec moi?"

"Bonjour, Cheni," répond Frémi. "Je ne peux pas jouer maintenant. Toute la famille travaille par ce beau temps. Nous nous préparons pour l'hiver qui reviendra bientôt. Au revoir."

Cheni continue son exploration du pommier. Tout à coup, elle entend un nouveau son. Elle écoute attentivement.

"Tsi, tsi, tsi! Tsi, tsi, tsi!"

Cheni se demande ce qui peut chanter de telle façon. Tout de même, elle décide qu'il lui vaut mieux être prudente. Elle se cache sous une feuille en attendant de voir qui est l'auteur de cette nouvelle chanson. Elle n'a pas long à attendre. Quelques instants plus tard, elle aperçoit Mitsi, la mésange, qui sautille de branche en branche à la recherche de son déjeuner. Quoique Cheni voudrait bien demander à Mitsi de jouer avec elle, quelque chose en elle-même lui assure que cela ne serait pas une bonne idée.

Peu après, Mitsi se dirige vers un autre pommier et Cheni est libre de continuer son chemin. De temps en temps, elle s'arrête pour goûter une feuille qui lui paraît plus appétissante que les autres. De temps à autre, elle revoit ses amis, Abi, Bouzi et Frémi, qui font le va-et-vient en travaillant; et c'est ainsi que la journée se passe.

Vers le coucher du soleil, Cheni se trouve sur la branche la plus haute du pommier. Les rayons du soleil couchant font briller les superbes pommes rouges qui pendent aux branches du pommier. Cheni en choisit une qui lui plaît et commence tout de suite à s'y ronger une maison.

Un peu plus tard, la nuit est tombée. La lune illumine les pommiers. Ses rayons pâles se reflètent dans la rosée qui couvre l'herbe du verger et c'est ainsi qu'on dirait qu'il y a un ciel étoilé sous les arbres. Quand Houbou, le hibou, passe par là à la recherche de son souper, il ne voit pas Cheni car elle est maintenant endormie dans sa nouvelle maison à l'intérieur d'une belle pomme rouge.

Maintenant, l'hiver peut venir. Cheni sera prête.

Donc, si vous allez dans un verger pour cueillir des pommes; faites attention. Examinez bien chacun des fruits que vous cueillez. Si vous y voyez un tout petit trou, il se peut bien que vous teniez la maison de Cheni à la main.

NANOR

There once was a frog who did not believe that he should be a frog. As such, he told his friends but not his relatives, for he had none of the latter, that he would someday leave them and their beloved swamp.

The frog's name was Nanor, pronounced [**nah-nor**]. It was not really such a spectacular or very different name and the other frogs did not think much of it. However, Nanor felt that his name was indeed very significant although he could not really explain why he felt as he did.

Nanor continually tried to tell anyone willing to listen that he had come to the swamp through very unusual circumstances. Whenever he would tell of how he firmly believed that in his previous life he had been a handsome young man with some importance in his community, the other frogs would break out in laughter.

"Ho! Ho! Ho!" laughed the large frogs.

"Ha! Ha! Ha!" laughed the medium-sized frogs.

"Hee! Hee! Hee!" laughed the small frogs.

Although Nanor felt sad because the other frogs did not believe his story, he never gave up hope that someday he would once again be a man and that he would be able to continue the life that he had left so many years before.

You may be wondering what kind of story Nanor told anyone who would listen; so I will tell you the way that he told it.

Whenever someone was willing to listen, Nanor, the frog, would begin his tale and continue as follows:

"A long time ago, I lived in a small village with my parents and my brothers and sisters. My father who was known as Master Ronan, pronounced **[Row-nahn]**, had been appointed leader of the village. It was his responsibility to make sure that all went well with all the people and the animals living there. My father was a just man. He ensured that everyone had enough to eat as well as a comfortable place to rest at night or to seek shelter when the wild storms blew in from the north country. Even though my father was the recognized leader of the village, our family lived much as did the rest of the community. Each adult member of the village had a job to do. Children began to help when they were still quite young. It made each person happy to know that he or she was a useful, contributing member of the community.

For many years, our village lived in peace and contentment. I grew up following in my father's footsteps. I learned how to understand those who lived around me. I learned how each person is different and has something unique to offer. As the years went by, I began to see how there are usually several ways of looking at problems and situations. I saw that it was good to look at things from a variety of points of view before making a choice or deciding an important matter.

The years went by. Eventually, my father grew old and the people of the village appointed me to look after them the way my father had done.

I continued the leadership that my father had shown. One day, however, things changed suddenly. A neighbouring village leader had decided that he should lead our community as well as his own. He came dressed in flashy clothing and accompanied by a band of musicians. The colours were bright, the music was loud, and to make things even worse, my rival leader handed out free ale to all who would have it. Before long, there was dancing, singing, and yelling in the streets of our peaceful village. I could see what was going to happen. I pleaded with the people not to be taken in by the flashy newcomer. Few listened however, and soon my rival began to speak. He promised great things for our village. The people began to yell encouragement, to cheer, and to applaud. In desperation, I demanded a chance to be heard. To my surprise, the new arrival granted me permission to speak.

Unaware of the evil intent of my rival, I jumped at the chance to address my fellow villagers. My heart was bursting with what I wanted to express to them. I reminded them of all that we had accomplished. I tried to make them see that it would be hard to find anyone in the village that was truly unhappy. As I spoke, I grew thirsty and asked for a glass of water. It was brought to me by one of my rival's servants. As soon as the water touched my tongue, I felt myself grow small. I went to get up but all I managed was a hop. It was then that I realized what had happened. I had been turned into a frog!

Most of the people watching were so excited and caught up by the newcomer's charm that they did not even notice my disappearance. I had no choice but to seek a new home. This is the way that I came to live in this lovely swamp with you, my friends."

This is the story that Nanor, the frog, told. Unfortunately, every time he told it, the same thing happened:

"Ho! Ho! Ho!" laughed the large frogs.

"Ha! Ha! Ha!" laughed the medium-sized frogs.

"Hee! Hee! Hee!" laughed the small frogs.

This went on for quite some time. Nanor was getting tired of telling his story and being made fun of. One day, he had an idea. He knew that all of the animals in the area truly respected

Houbou, pronounced [**oo-boo**], the wise owl who made his home in one of the hollow trees of the swamp. Nanor decided to ask Houbou to verify his story. Everyone knew that Houbou knew everything that went on in the swamp and its surroundings. It was also common knowledge that the wise owl was very, very old and that he knew a great deal about local history.

Thus it came about that one evening when the fat moon sailed through a cloudless summer sky, Houbou came to address the frogs of the swamp. The story that he had to tell was very much the same as the one that Nanor had told time and time again. The wise owl spoke in a solemn voice and when he was finished, not a single frog laughed. In fact, the swamp had never been so quiet. After a short time, little by little, each of the frogs that lived in the swamp came by to apologize to Nanor. The way of life that he had learned as a child had not been forgotten by Nanor and he accepted the apologies with forgiveness and understanding.

So it came to be that the attitude of the frogs of the swamp changed towards Nanor.

Each member of the swamp community wanted to help him if it were possible. However, not a single frog knew what to do to restore Nanor to his former shape and stature.

Meanwhile, Houbou the owl had watched what was going on. One evening, he spoke as follows:

"I know someone living in the nearby forest who may be able to help. She is a very kind magician. Gwendolyn of the Trees is her name. She would not refuse to help us if she can. Of that I am certain."

The following evening, Houbou came back with news.

"The lovely magician, Gwendolyn, says that you must be able to ride a horse back to the village, Nanor. Once there, if you jump in the arms of the evil leader's daughter, Isabelle, you will regain your human form."

At these words, the frogs began to moan in despair for all knew that frogs do not ride horses. Nanor, however, became full of hope. He thanked Houbou and immediately began to think of a plan that would restore him to the people of his village.

It was known that the evil leader and his men often came by the swamp on their way to the forest to hunt. Nanor knew that his only chance was to jump on a horse as it went by. He knew that from the ground, this was not possible. That is why the rest of the frogs were sad and had given up hope. Nanor, in spite of this, had an idea: He would climb a tree.

Imagine the reaction of the frogs when they heard his idea. A frog climb a tree!

"Ho! Ho! Ho!" laughed the large frogs.

"Ha! Ha! Ha!" laughed the medium-sized frogs.

"Hee! Hee! Hee!" laughed the small frogs.

Nanor was not discouraged. He began to practice immediately; and one day, he found himself so high in a tree that he could see his village in the distance. As he watched, he saw in a cloud of dust the evil leader and his men approaching on their horses. Nanor was in a tree just above the path that the horsemen were following. As the leader's horse went by, Nanor jumped unnoticed in the leader's hunting bag.

Nanor had always loved all the animals of the forest and it was with sincere hope that he prayed that the leader and his hunters would find nothing to shoot that day. As darkness was beginning to fall and the hunters, hungry and tired, had found nothing; the leader gave orders to return to the village.

The horsemen galloped back to their homes and as the leader entered his own house, he threw his hunting bag on the table in disgust. His daughter, sitting at the table, was secretly pleased for she was a kind soul who loved life and all that it has to offer. She did not approve of her father's ways. His hunting of the animals of the forest had always made her sad.

It was at this point that Nanor jumped out of the bag and into the arms of the evil leader's daughter. Instantly, Nanor returned to his former shape. As he did, he apologized for intruding so rudely upon the young woman's space. She, however, did not seem displeased at all. On the other hand, her father immediately recognized the young man as the young Master Ronan. He was so shocked that he fell into a long sleep. As far as I know, he has not yet awakened from it.

So it came about that Nanor became once more Master Ronan. The frogs of the swamp understood why their friend had thought that his name was significant. The better spellers among them realized that "Nanor" was "Ronan" spelled backwards. They had also learned from him that one should never give up hope. The old proverb "where there is a will there is a way" had certainly been proven true by Nanor, the frog.

The young Master Nanor restored the previous order to his village. He made certain that everyone was able to feel necessary to the community. Everyone felt that he or she had something to offer no matter how different he or she might be from his or her friends and relatives.

I have been told that Ronan and Isabelle (as you will recall, that is the lovely daughter's name) now have a family.

And oh, how their children love to hear the story of their father's adventure. Believe me, no one laughs when he tells it.

It has also come to my attention that Ronan, after discussion with the people of the village, and much to the delight of the frogs and the animals, has declared that the swamp and the forest are now a public park where no hunting is allowed.

I suppose that if you want to pay a visit to the village that I have just told you about, it could be arranged; particularly if you have a good imagination.

Oh, by the way, now you also know where tree frogs got their start.

THE GLITCH – ENCOUNTER ONE

The last few hours have been out of this world and into another or vice versa. I am not sure. It all started innocently enough as most nightmares do. Right now, it looks as though I have a few minutes to enter this in my portable voice-activated microprocessor. It is a neat gadget. You tell it what you want, it writes to a memory stick and later, you copy the data to your computer's hard drive and get a hard copy printout or do whatever you want with it. For someone like me who likes to dabble in a little writing, it's perfect for recording ideas whenever or wherever they occur. So you see, if I seem a little wordy and maybe more than a little disorganized in my report to you, it's because this is off the top of my head as I recall it.

In any case, let me tell you a little about myself. My name is Gerald Awrey. When I was a kid in school, once in a while, others would call me Ger the bear, Gerry the Berry and sometimes Geronimo, which I didn't really mind. I've been called a lot worse. I have a PhD in music and so there are some people who can't stop themselves from calling me Doctor Awrey. I prefer Gerry or even better, as Lana calls me,

Ger. No doubt now you're going to wonder who this Lana is. I'll tell you about her in a moment. As I was saying, I'm into music. For the past two years, I have been working for Musictech, a company that sells its ideas to established musicians who can afford it. Rock groups are regular customers. My job is to write music with the help of a specially programmed computer. I thoroughly enjoy my work. Most musicians use my computerized musical composition as a starting point. However, if you'll pardon my bragging a little, I have heard some tunes on the radio that were largely unchanged from the manner in which I had composed the original.

Now, you are probably wondering about Lana. Lana joined the company as a student apprentice six months ago. At first, I thought that she would be more of a bother than was worth it and I must be honest and tell you that I protested her proposed apprenticeship with me. I prefer to work alone; I've always enjoyed my privacy and I don't mind telling you that I've always been thought of as somewhat of a loner. However, the company was adamant and so there I was with a pretty assistant albeit an undesired one.

Lana soon changed my mind about a lot of things. It took no time at all for me to discover that she was intelligent, conscientious and hard-working. She was neat, punctual and reliable, all of which are qualities that I have always valued.

In case some of you are jumping to conclusions about our relationship, you should know that Lana is twenty-two years old and I am twenty years her senior which makes me old enough to be her father. Moreover, I must admit that I have always been a little intimidated by beautiful women. I was married to one and I believe that if she had not been so young at the time that I met her for the first time, I would never have found enough courage to ask her out on a date. Now I'll have you wondering what happened to the first and only wife I've ever had.

All right, I'll explain. Her first name is Phyllis but she prefers to go by her second which is Lee. I think Phyllis is a great name so I often would tease her by using that name and she would get angry with me. She used to say that I was good at teasing; I just didn't know when to do it and when not to. Lee is a beautiful, intelligent woman. I think the reason that we are no longer together is that we are so different in our needs, desires and priorities.

For example, I am quite content to wander about my back lot trimming a bush here, pruning a tree there, watching the birds, tending to my grapevines or tilling the garden. Lee would rather be on the move doing something exciting. I don't blame her. We're different, that's all. We felt that we were a little too dissimilar to try and pretend we could have a genuinely happy life together so we made what we think is a smart decision. We have been apart for three years now and we are still best friends. I love her and I know I always will. We have three wonderful children to show for our time together and that is more than a lot of couples would ask for.

So much for the preliminaries. I mentioned at the start of my narration that I think that this may be a nightmare. I know it doesn't much sound like one so far but you be the judge and decide whether or not at least some parts of my experience are worthy of this classification. You should also know that, at this point, I'm still not certain where I am.

This is the way it all began.

When I came into the lab this morning, Lana was already at work. We were just finishing up a piece of music that was to be shipped by one o'clock this afternoon. Lana appeared to be extremely frustrated.

"What's the matter?" I asked.

"Oh, hell, Ger. I can't get this note off the screen. It simply won't delete no matter what I do. I've tried everything, warm boot, cold boot, reset; I've even used the special deletion program that we installed last month; nothing works. This is one stubborn note."

"Let me have a look. Where's the cursor?"

"That's just it, there isn't one. It's as if the note has covered it up or swallowed it or something."

I could not believe this so I tried the same things that Lana had done up to that point. Nothing worked. The note remained intact no matter what I tried.

I was getting angry. "If this is those computer nerds' idea of a joke, it's the last time they'll ever set foot in this lab."

"You mean those guys from the university? No way, they're not even allowed to touch this unit anyway. I know they've got a weird sense of humor but I don't think they would do something like this."

"Well, you explain it then, **Ms. Loren**! What the hell are we supposed to do now? You tell me! This piece has to be ready in four hours and we're not even half finished yet!"

She didn't answer. There was no point. I was angry and it wasn't her fault. I was falling into one of my old habits, looking for someone else to blame when something goes wrong. I'd apologize..., later. For now, I felt there was only one thing left to do. We had enough of the work saved to be able to finish the job even if we lost the work that Lana had done that morning.

"I'm going to format this section of the program, Lana. It's the only way I can think of to get rid of this glitch. If we hurry, we've got enough done already to still be able to finish before the deadline. Listen, I'm sorry about the work that you've done today being lost and I'm sorry about snapping at you earlier. I know I can be a real jerk now and then."

"Don't worry about it. I'll get the backup disk."

"Thanks. Here goes."

This is when things began to get strange. The instant I started the formatting function, large letters appeared on the screen:

DO NOT ATTEMPT TO DELETE THE ENTITY!

"What is **this**?!? It's got to be those morons from UCV. Wait until I get my hands on them!"

I tried once more. This time, not only did the letters appear on the screen but a voice that sounded neither male nor female came through the speakers:

"DO...NOT.......ATTEMPT..TO......DELETE...THE.......ENTITY!"

"I can't believe this crap! Those computer cretins have even had time to do this!?!"

"Ger, I really don't think they would do something like this even if they could, and I doubt that very much."

"Well, all right. There's only one other thing I can think of. We're going to physically remove a chip. We're going in, Lana."

Again, the voice and the letters simultaneously expressed their warning, this time with a little more threat implied:

"IF...YOU.......ATTEMPT.......FURTHER..TO...DESTROY...THE......ENTITY
..WE...WILL..BE......FORCED..TO....TAKE.......ACTION!

"Entity, my ass. Sorry, Lana. If this is an entity, I'm Superman and you're Lois Lane. Those dimwits are in serious trouble, Lana. You wait and see."

I took a screwdriver from Lana, bent down to open the computer case and that was when I felt more than heard something behind us. I looked up. Lana's mouth was wide open and it looked as though she were seeing a ghost and maybe she was, I'm still not sure about that. Standing by the door were two "beings." I don't know what else to call them.

They seemed to be neither male nor female and when they spoke the voice was the same as the one that had come through the speakers earlier. They reminded me a little of Data from Star Trek except that they were dressed in an unrecognizable material and manner. They began to speak:

"YOUR.......ACTIONS.....LEAVE..US..NO......CHOICE...YOU....WILL.. ..COME....WITH..US...YOU....MUST..BE.........PROCESSED."

I think that's the point at which I began to think I was dreaming. I expected to wake up at any moment. The strange thing is that I have awakened; at least I think I have. One thing is for sure, I'm not in the lab. In fact, I'm not sure where I am. And until a few moments ago, I didn't know if Lana was part of this particular segment of the weird experience. I'll tell you about that in a moment.

The room I'm in is not like any I've ever been in before. The material for the floor, the walls and the ceiling appears to be all the same. It feels firm but soft at the same time. It is very comfortable to sit on, lie on or walk on. There is nothing in the room. The air is fresh and the light seems to come from everywhere at once. I would absolutely believe myself in a dream if I hadn't seen what I saw a few moments ago with my own eyes. Mind you, what does that prove?

A short while ago, one of the beings came into the room. I asked him or her or it (I'll refer to it as a "he", it's easier that way) where I was and whether or not Lana was here as well. He told me in that same hesitant but very clear neutral voice that I would find out everything shortly. Lana was being "processed" and I would see her in a moment. Sure enough, almost as he finished speaking, Lana appeared.

"They don't wear clothing here," she said with a smile. "I'll see you later."

I was too stunned to say anything. I knew she was beautiful but I hadn't expected her to suddenly appear before me as naked as a newborn babe. Another strange thing for me, I did not feel embarrassed, although I have to admit that I was taken aback a little.

So now, I'm waiting here. I still haven't figured out whether this is a dream or a nightmare. This last part about Lana certainly doesn't feel much like a nightmare should. Perhaps I'll wake up before being "processed." At this point, I don't know if I would be relieved or disappointed.

NESS

People call me Ness. Those who think they are my friends call me Nessie. It's ironic. They give me the name of the monster from Loch Ness. They have no idea how close they are to the monster within me. It's not even my first name.

I've been on the street for quite a few years now. I have no idea who my father was and my mother literally threw me out of the house when I was fourteen years of age. She did it after I completely destroyed one of her boyfriends who thought he would get his way with me. Something happened within me and I looked right into his eyes and he went crazy. I'd never seen anyone so afraid. He's now spending his days babbling in some psychiatric ward.

I knew from that moment that I have a gift. It's not so bad on the street at all. With my gift, I can get whatever I want. I don't abuse it. The abusers though, are getting fewer by the day around these parts. I'm pretty and young and they are attracted to me. I can read through their thoughts. I wait for just the right moment and look right into their eyes. That is all. They become insane and will not abuse anyone any time soon.

I am grateful for my gift. By the way, my first name has always been **Dark**.

OUBI

Oubi est un petit ours qui habite dans une région bien loin de chez nous. C'est le pays des ours. Ce pays s'appelle la Noursonie.

Oubi est un jeune ours bien ordinaire; comme vous et comme moi. Il n'est pas parfait. Il fait des gaffes lui aussi, tout comme vous et tout comme moi. Il voudrait bien toujours faire ce qui est bon mais, assez souvent, il sait que ce qu'il vient de faire n'est pas ce qu'il aurait dû faire. Comme vous pouvez voir, il est bien comme moi et bien comme vous.

Ce matin, il fait très beau. Le soleil brille dans un ciel bleu de printemps. Les oiseaux chantent dans le nouveau feuillage des arbres verts. Les abeilles bourdonnent en travaillant parmi les nouvelles fleurs. Et quelles fleurs! Il y en a de toutes les couleurs. Et quel parfum elles donnent à leur entourage!

Oubi sort de chez lui. Sa mère lui a dit d'aller cueillir de nouvelles fraises qu'elle a aperçues le jour précédant au bord de la forêt. "Ne va pas près de la rivière car cela pourrait être dangereux," lui a dit sa mère.

Oubi est rempli de bonnes intentions. Il prend son panier et se dirige vers la clairière décrite par sa mère. Il ne se presse pas. Il respire l'air frais. Il écoute les oiseaux. Il regarde les abeilles travailler. Il s'arrête ici et là pour sentir les fleurs. Il dit bonjour à tout ceux et celles qu'il rencontre. Il se dit qu'il a bien assez de temps pour cueillir les fraises que sa maman lui a demandé de cueillir.

Peu à peu Oubi s'approche du champ de fraises. Tout à coup, le murmure de la rivière se fait entendre et cela rappelle à notre ami les beaux poissons qui doivent y attendre à être pris. Oubi a déjà vu son père et sa mère prendre des poissons. Il y a longtemps qu'il veut aller à la pêche, lui aussi. Malheureusement, ses parents le croient encore trop jeune.

Que faire? La rivière semble l'appeler:

"Oubi! Oubi! Viens vite! Les poissons sont là. Ils t'attendent. Tu n'as qu'à venir les prendre."

Oubi est troublé. D'un côté, il sait bien qu'il devrait faire ce que sa mère lui a dit de faire. D'un autre côté, dans son imagination, il peut déjà voir les magnifiques poissons nager dans l'eau claire de la rivière. Il est absolument certain qu'il peut en prendre au moins un ou deux s'en trop s'attarder.

Oubi se dit, "Il est encore tôt. J'ai bien assez de temps pour cueillir les fraises avant le coucher du soleil. Comme il fait chaud! Qu'il me serait agréable de me mettre les pattes dans l'eau fraîche de la rivière! De plus, je crois bien que Papa et Maman seraient fiers de moi si je leur apportais quelques gros poissons pour notre dîner. Bon! C'en est fait! Je vais à la pêche!"

Oubi pose son panier au pied d'un arbre. Il s'approche de la rivière. Plus il s'approche, plus il est agité. Une fois rendu au bord de l'eau, il voit que pour essayer de prendre les poissons, il doit aller plus loin, vers le milieu de la rivière.

Oubi se décide. Il descend dans l'eau. L'eau est très froide mais il sait ce qu'il veut faire. Il continue à s'avancer. Tout à coup, ses pieds ne touchent plus le fond et il s'enfonce sous l'eau! Oubi est saisi de terreur. Le courant de la rivière est bien fort et il s'empare de notre ami et l'emporte. Après quelques instants de panique, Oubi remonte à la surface et crie de toutes ses forces; mais personne ne l'entend. Quelques instants plus tard, Oubi aperçoit un tronc d'arbre qui vient vers lui. Il s'y accroche et la rivière l'emmène de plus en plus loin de chez lui.

Plus le temps passe, plus la rivière s'élargit et plus le paysage change. Après plusieurs heures, accroché à l'arbre flottant, Oubi se rend compte qu'il est maintenant très loin de sa maison. Les montagnes ne sont plus là. Les arbres de plus en plus s'éloignent de la rivière et on peut voir de temps à autre une habitation humaine ici et là. Oubi reconnaît bien ses maisons qui servent de logis aux êtres qui marchent sur deux jambes car ses parents lui en ont parlé plusieurs fois depuis son arrivée dans le monde.

Le soleil rougit et peu à peu disparaît derrière les arbres qui bordent la rivière. Lentement, le soir passe et la nuit tombe. Les étoiles apparaissent dans le ciel et bientôt la lune se montre au dessus des champs bordant maintenant la rivière devenue fleuve.

Oubi voit bien qu'il s'éloigne de plus en plus de la rive. Il sait que s'il ne fait aucun effort, il sera bientôt trop loin pour essayer de faire ce qu'il a jusqu'ici toujours eu peur d'essayer.

"Je dois nager!" se dit-il. Il se souvient très bien que ses parents lui ont dit maintes fois que les ours savent nager tout naturellement. Malheureusement, il n'a jamais voulu les laisser lui montrer comment cela se fait; et maintenant, il se doit bien d'essayer de nager sans que personne ne puisse lui venir en aide.

Oubi se détache de l'arbre. Il commence tout de suite à nager avec ses quatre pattes. Il est soulagé de voir qu'il ne s'enfonce pas sous l'eau. Peu à peu, il s'approche du rivage. Lorsqu'il parvient à mettre pieds sur terre ferme, la lune est déjà bien haute dans le ciel. Oubi a froid, il est seul, il est bien triste et s'il doit se l'admettre, il a un peu peur. Il croit entendre Houbou, le hibou sage le gronder:

"Hou! Hou! Tu aurais dû écouter ta maman, mon petit."

"Oui, c'est vrai. J'aurais bien dû écouter Maman!" soupire Oubi.

La lune continue son trajet dans le ciel. Il commence à faire assez froid pour qu'une petite gelée commence à se faire voir sur la nouvelle herbe. Oubi sait que pour rejoindre la Noursonie, il doit se mettre à marcher vers le nord car c'est là où se trouve sa demeure. Il commence à marcher même s'il est épuisé et presque à bout de forces. La lumière de la lune éclaire son chemin. De temps en temps, Oubi entend les aboiements des chiens d'une ferme voisine. Il fait de son mieux pour ne pas faire de bruit car il ne veut pas attirer l'attention de ces amis des hommes.

Les heures passent. Oubi est maintenant si fatigué qu'il décide enfin de s'allonger un peu pour se reposer. Il trouve un bosquet épais où il s'endort presque tout de suite.

Pendant que notre ami dort, la lune continue son chemin vers l'ouest. Bientôt, elle pâlit et disparaît derrière les collines. À l'est, le ciel rose se prépare à recevoir le soleil. Peu à peu, les premiers rayons du soleil printanier réussissent à pénétrer dans les buissons où dort le petit ours. Un de ces rayons particulièrement insistant semble dire, "Oubi! Oubi! Réveille-toi!" et enfin, Oubi ouvre les yeux. Pendant quelques instants, il ne sait pas où il se trouve. Tout de même, après peu de temps, il se souvient de son aventure de la veille.

Oubi a très faim. Malheureusement. à peine a-t-il le temps de penser à se trouver quelque chose à manger qu'il entend des aboiements qui s'approchent. Les chiens de la ferme non loin de là ont dû trouver sa piste et maintenant, ils sont à sa poursuite.

Oubi court aussi vite que ses petites pattes peuvent le porter mais les chiens sont plus rapides que lui. Notre petit ami sait maintenant qu'il ne pourra pas échapper à ses ennemis à moins d'un miracle. Il ne peut plus courir. Que va-t-il faire?

Soudain, Oubi croit entendre quelque chose. Il écoute. C'est la rivière qui l'appelle:

"Oubi! Oubi! Saute dans l'eau! Nage! Les chiens ne t'y suivront pas!" lui dit-elle.

"Tu as raison. Je n'ai pas le choix," répond Oubi.

Sans plus hésiter, Oubi entre dans l'eau et commence à nager vers le centre de la rivière juste au moment où les chiens sortent du bois. Ils aboient, hurlent, et gémissent mais ils n'osent pas poursuivre le petit ours dans l'eau. Peu à peu, Oubi s'éloigne et les chiens, fatigués de la poursuite inutile, retournent lentement chez eux.

Petit à petit, Oubi se rapproche du rivage et bientôt, il est de retour dans la forêt. Ici et là, il trouve quelque petits fruits forestiers pour appaiser sa faim. Après plusieurs heures de marche, il commence à reconnaître le paysage d'où il est venu.

Le soleil a déjà commencé sa descente quand Oubi apperçoit enfin son panier qu'il avait laissé au pied d'un arbre. Il se dépêche à trouver la clairière où se trouvent les fraises. En peu de temps, son panier est rempli de délicieuses fraises rouges et juteuses. Comme Oubi a envie de toutes les manger! Mais il veut réparer son erreur - la peine qu'il a causée à ses parents par sa désobéissance; donc il se dépêche à rentrer chez lui.

Immaginez la surprise et le soulagement de ses parents lorsqu'ils voient leur cher Oubi courir vers eux, panier de fraises à la main, après un retard d'une longue nuit et d'une interminable journée. Ils sont si heureux de le voir qu'ils n'ont pas la volonté de le punir. De plus, les explications de leur fils suffisent à les persuader qu'il a appris une leçon qu'il n'est pas à la veille d'oublier.

C'est pour cela que si vous visitez la Noursonie, vous verrez peut-être Oubi à la pêche; mais vous pouvez être certains qu'il y sera avec la permission de ses parents. Et tant qu'il sera trop jeune pour aller tout seul à la pêche, vous pouvez être sûrs que lorsqu'il sera à patauger dans sa rivière préférée, ni son père ni sa mère ne seront loin de là.

Pourquoi la Girafe a un Long Cou

C'était il y a bien longtemps. Le soleil, la lune et la terre étaient tous encore bien jeunes. Au temps duquel je vous parle, le soleil étant fatigué de voyager seul dans le ciel avait décidé de se trouver une épouse. La lune, la déesse de la nuit lui paraissait si belle, bien que timide, qu'il lui semblait qu'elle serait une bonne compagne. Il s'était donc décidé de la convaincre de l'épouser.

Je crois bien que tout se serait bien passé si Madame Curiosité n'avait pas rendu visite à la girafe. Malheureusement pour le soleil, c'est exactement ce qui se passa un beau jour.

En ce temps-là, la girafe avait un cou "normal". Il n'était pas plus long que ni le tien ni le mien. Mais après la visite de Mme Curiosité, vous allez vous rendre compte que tout cela a changé.

Pendant sa visite avec la girafe, Mme Curiosité n'arrêtait pas de faire celle-là poser des questions telles que: Qui...? Où...? Comment...? Pourquoi...? Quand...? Depuis quand...? Si bien qu'à la longue, il en vient que la girafe voulut vraiment savoir ce que le soleil voulait de Mademoiselle la Lune.

C'est ainsi que dès le lendemain matin, la girafe se leva et alla tout de suite à la rencontre du soleil qui se levait et s'en allait gentiment à la poursuite de la lune timide. Lorsque celle-ci vit que la girafe observait ce qui allait se passer entre le soleil et elle-même, elle s'enfuit lentement vers l'ouest et disparut.

Ce soir-là, le soleil frustré se coucha tandis que la girafe essayait de s'allonger le cou au maximum pour voir ce qui se passerait peut-être de l'autre côté de l'horizon. Le soleil, voyant ceci, devint rouge de colère et le ciel en fut son témoin.

Le lendemain matin, la même chose se répéta. Lorsque le soleil voulut s'approcher de Mademoiselle la Lune, il vit que la girafe les regardait avec intérêt; et lorsque la lune remarqua la curieuse, elle partit lentement vers l'horizon de l'ouest et encore une fois disparut.

Il en fut ainsi pendant les sept prochains jours. Tous les matins, le soleil se levait espérant parler à la femme de ses rêves, mais dès qu'il regardait vers la terre, il voyait la girafe qui s'allongeait le cou en l'observant avec intérêt et curiosité. Il put voir que le cou de la girafe continuait de s'allonger de jour en jour.

À bout de sa patience, le soleil eut une idée. Il demanda aux nuages de couvrir la terre afin que la girafe ne puisse pas le voir essayer de convaincre la lune de se joindre à lui. Les nuages en furent d'accord et bientôt ils recouvrirent le ciel. Tout était sombre sur la terre.

Ce matin-là, lorsque la girafe s'éveilla; elle vit le ciel gris et sombre pour la première fois. Curieuse, elle leva la tête et étira son cou si bien que bientôt elle put voir au-dessus des nuages. Dès que la lune vit la girafe qui les regardait, elle et l'astre du jour; elle continua son chemin vers l'ouest et bientôt disparut encore une fois.

Quand le soleil se rendit compte de ce qui s'était passé, il fut si malheureux qu'il se mit à pleurer. Il continua ainsi pendant plusieurs jours. Sur la terre, tout était sombre et la pluie ne cessait de tomber. Il se forma des ruisseaux, des étangs, des rivières, des lacs, des mers, et bientôt des océans. Après un mois à peu près, la terre entière était presque complètement couverte d'eau.

Enfin, le soleil entendit les plaintes des êtres qui habitaient sur la terre. Il eut pitié d'eux, même de la girafe; car il se rendit compte que, sans la visite de Mme Curiosité, la girafe ne lui aurait jamais causé de misère. Ce n'était pas qu'elle voulait lui faire du mal, c'était que la curiosité faisait maintenant partie de son caractère.

C'est alors que le soleil cessa de pleurer. Le niveau de l'eau sur la terre descendit peu à peu jusqu'au moment où il n'y resta que ruisseaux, étangs, rivières, lacs, mers, et océans.

Depuis ce temps, le soleil a cessé de poursuivre la lune pour s'approcher d'elle. Il se contente de la suivre de l'est à l'ouest chaque jour.

La girafe, elle, a toujours le cou long. Elle a oublié pourquoi. Néanmoins, elle s'en sert pour manger les feuilles succulentes du haut des arbres.

Quelquefois, quand le soleil se souvient de ce qui s'est passé, il chauffe le pays de la girafe un peu trop longtemps. De temps en temps, il est triste de ne pas avoir pu épouser sa bonne amie et c'est ainsi que le ciel pleure par la pluie; et la terre, que la lune aime regarder, reverdit. Et quand le soleil voit son amie sourire, il caresse la pluie et les nuages de ses rayons et ceux-ci dessinent un arc-en-ciel dans le ciel.

Maintenant, vous savez pourquoi la girafe a le cou long, vous savez d'où vient l'arc-en-ciel, vous savez pourquoi il pleut, et vous comprenez aussi pourquoi, par respect, on appelle la lune, Madame la Lune.

Bon, voilà. Mon histoire est finie. Je ne suis pas certain qu'elle soit exactement juste. De toutes façons, il se fait tard.

C'est le temps de se mettre au lit. Bonsoir à Madame la Lune et à vous tous qui aimez les histoires.

PAPA'S GIRL

Not too long ago, I had a dream. It was a dream in which I was with a little girl; I assume she was my daughter. I already have a very fine, intelligent, and lovely son and two lovely, fine, and intelligent daughters so I do not know why I would have this intensely loving, protective, and proud feeling about having another child; but that is certainly the way I felt.

In any event, in the dream in question, I find myself proudly parading this little girl (no specific name comes to mind but she is probably between four and six years old) around a town that seems oddly dated; like something out of the late 1800's. We are holding hands and walking slowly down what I presume to be the main, and perhaps the only, street in town. People nod and smile in approval. The little girl is dressed as though we might be going to church or to a birthday party or some special occasion. She is wearing a pink dress, white stockings and white shoes. I feel this intense sense of pride and protectiveness.

(At this point in the dream, I awoke. I felt a great sense of loss and immediately willed myself back to sleep. As has

happened to me before, I was immensely relieved to find myself back in the dream.)

The little girl and I are still walking slowly and eventually come to the end of the street past this building that seems to be completely open to the street. I see a shop where my father is working. He nods and smiles. In what seems to be a family room, I sense a sibling but although I feel whom he might be (I have six in real life,) I cannot make him out so I am not sure how he feels. Then, in what appears to be the kitchen, I see my mother. She also nods and acknowledges our presence but just stands there.

(Dreams are much like movies sometimes. They use cinematographic techniques such as flashback and foreshadowing and time seems quite meaningless.)

The little girl and I are now on a high wooden platform with no railing. It is above railroad tracks. She is thrilled and runs and skips back and forth as she clearly loves to hear the tapping sound of her shoes on the wooden boards. Suddenly, she seems to lose her balance and to my horror, I see that she is about to fall off the platform. It seems that I am too far to catch her but just before the dream can become a nightmare, I am able to catch her and prevent her fall. I can feel the anguish, the fear, the beating of my heart, and an immense and benevolent sense of relief.

(Fade in a new scene...)

The little girl and I are now on the ground by the railroad tracks. There is a sense of happiness and peace again. We see an approaching train. It is old. It has a steam locomotive. People are leaning out the windows and waving at us. The little girl and I, still holding hands walk toward the train.

(That was the end of the dream. At this point, I woke up and it was actually time to get on with my day. I felt very good inside.)

PS: It is interesting to me that at no point in this dream is there any sign nor feeling of a mother in the picture at all. Again, this is odd since my children have a great mom with whom I remain friends (although we have been divorced for quite some time).

The dream always makes me wonder about what marvellous and mysterious journey the little girl and I are about to embark upon.

This is an unforgettable and recurring dream to which there has been no conclusion so far. I hope this dream comes again. Come to think of it, perhaps in another dimension or another life, it is not a dream at all, but reality.

SUMMER SNOW

The man was awakened by the absence of habitual bird calls. Through his open bedroom window, he could hear nothing. He supposed that this was what had wakened him for he was a regular riser, beckoned from sleep in summer by the songs of his feathered friends. He forced himself from the bed and went to the window. The dawn sky was the colour of copper. As he looked to the east, he realized that the dawn was getting more sombre. And then, he heard it. It was an almost inaudible sound, a little like radio static at low volume. Something was falling from the sky through the leaves of the trees but it was not rain. He put his hand out the window and felt something like tiny broken bits of egg shells alighting on his exposed skin. He pulled his arm back into the room. It was covered with warm, snow-like flakes. He brought one to his tongue. It was salty. The hissing sound was growing louder and he looked once more out the window at the falling summer snow. He decided to close the window...

...Some two weeks later as the first of many villagers began to file past his house on the outskirts of the town; the man began to feel an undeniable, inner urge to go outside.

He was getting very thirsty. The water had become undrinkable some days ago and he had used up all the potable liquids in the house, including that in the toilet bowl. He stared at his fellow townspeople as they queued by. They seemed intent on going west. None spoke. They just stared ahead and trudged along. The man noted that there were no children and no one seemed to be much more than middle-aged. The others were already dead, he supposed...

...He thought back over the last couple of weeks. The silent white summer storm had been quite a phenomenon. The media had gone wild with speculation as to its cause. However, this frenzy of conjecture had soon come to an end as electrical power had begun to wane and, at last, gone out completely. The man had stayed indoors, afraid to go out into the snow of salt. Now, as he watched his fellow humans file past, the urge inside became strong enough to overcome his fear of venturing outside. He thought of the sea, some 200 kilometres to the west and his heart began to quicken its beat. He suddenly felt that he had a goal! He had a destination, he had a real purpose.

He opened the door and, almost fervently, took his place in the line of earthlings seeking their way to the ocean. He felt as though he were on a pilgrimage.

The first of the westward migratory folk began to stumble shortly before the sun set on that first day of the man's trek. It was not long before he had to avoid tripping over someone lying on the ground. He would have liked to have been of help, but what could he do? The sea beckoned more strongly than ever. Someone had to make it, and then, everything would be made right again.

Several hours later, after a night of walking, the man thought that he could hear the sound of waves. He couldn't be sure, however. The sun was now rising in a sky of surreal blue, almost too blue to be sky. He had become heedless of his thirst and aching muscles at some time during the night. But fatigue had crept up on him, and as he fell into the synthetic snow, it was a relief. He was getting tired of walking over dead and dying humanoids. It was time for a rest...

...He lay on his back. He could hear the sea. Couldn't he? Of course, it was the sea. And it was just over the next rise. He would just rest for a few moments and then he would get up and he would...

...He dozed and the dream came...

...He could see a bucket brigade of his fellow humans reaching all the way down to the sea. Someone had made it, perhaps it was he. The first would dip an empty ice cream pail into the sea, take a drink, and pass it back with the right hand. There would be an empty pail in his left hand ready to be filled and passed on back. It was beautiful, refreshing to see such cooperation, such purpose. And the line of hopefuls was endless. Perhaps it encircled the planet. The man could not be sure as the dream faded, but he smiled as the first circling shadow kissed his wrinkled face and the sound of the waves lulled him into sleep...

...He did not feel the tear of his flesh as the first vulture found purchase...

THE DITCH

I don't know why I am bothering to put this story on paper. I have a feeling that I won't get to finish it, and even if I do, I don't think anyone in his right mind is going to believe it.

But it's true. Every word of it!

Right now, as I write this, it is completely dark outside. Rain is falling, if you can call it rain. It is so heavy, so massive and so powerful that it feels as though the house were under a waterfall. And the wind! Just a moment ago the house shook; sitting here in front of the computer, I felt it.

Thump! There it goes again. I think it's the wind; I mean, what else could it be? I should go out and check but I admit it; I'm really quite afraid of going outside at night...

It wasn't always that way. Until quite recently even, I loved going out at night whether the weather was clear or foul; I didn't care. I loved walking about in the moonlight, listening to the sounds of the night. If it was raining or snowing, I thrilled at the feel of the rain or snow on my face. And I embraced the wind even as a child. I loved the wind!

But all that has changed now. Something sinister and unknown until now has made its way here. I think that it is evil but it isn't its fault. I feel that is its nature and it did not choose it. It is the product of a series of events leading to circumstances that those of us who get to survive for a while will live to regret.

I'm digressing. Let me start at the beginning.

I've lived here for nearly thirty years now. When I first came here, the land all around this place was pastoral in nature. It consisted primarily of dairy farms and lovely fields that produced crops. Over the years however, the pressures of the expanding city to the west began to be felt here. People seeking cheaper housing or hoping to enjoy a country lifestyle began to move to the nearby town. In a few years, development began in earnest. Soon, there were shopping malls, apartment buildings, condominiums and the inevitable first highrises. This in turn led to an incredible increase in the price of land; a speculator's dream, a developer's fantasy. Before long, farmland disappeared under the pavement of commercial and industrial establishments. The character of the whole region changed rapidly...

Thump! Thump! ... There's that noise again. The wind must be banging something against the sun deck. Yeah, that must be it.

Let's see. Where was I? Oh, yeah ... Because our farm is close to the freeway, it was one of the first affected. Some years ago, a truck stop was built just across the road from where we live. It was so successful that soon, there was another and then another and a little while later, yet another. There was money to be made and no fuel company wanted to be left out.

As a result of this, the pressure on the ecosystems surrounding the new commercial endeavours was soon felt. Nowhere was it more in evidence than in the drainage ditch that runs along the side of our property.

This ditch is the focal point of this narrative.

Before the development swallowed most of it in culverts beneath pavement, the ditch ran straight from the west for about one mile, before flowing into a marshy, meandering stream which in turn made its way to a mighty river a few kilometres downstream. Also before the madness of development descended on the area, the ditch and the stream were home to all kinds of wildlife ranging in species from frogs and fish to great blue herons. The spring evenings and nights were filled with the songs from choruses of frogs. Ducks -- mallards, teals, wood ducks, and even wild geese made the ditch and the surrounding woods and brush their home. Some raised their young there during the spring and summer while others were only wintering visitors. Herons were familiar visitors while raccoons, coyotes, foxes, opossums, and even deer were common to the area.

All was changed one day about five years ago. I had gone for a walk in the woods behind the house. On my way back, I decided to return along the ditch. I was not prepared for what my eyes would see. Everywhere along both sides of the watercourse, the grasses were dead. It appeared as though the vegetation along the ditch had been sprayed by a powerful herbicide. All the greenery that had come in contact with the water was burned!

I ran home to call the "authorities". It was discovered that the culprit was run-off from the nearby fuel stations; obviously, great quantities of diesel fuel were entering the drainage ditch and this toxic substance was making its way to the stream and eventually to the river.

There followed three years of investigation, tests, and reports. Meanwhile the pollution continued and the ecosystem sustained more and more damage. Eventually, I got tired of dealing with the "proper channels" and I contacted the media. Once the story made the local papers, things changed. A date was soon set for a trial which would determine the degree of guilt that the offending companies were to bear. The trial ensued and although the fines handed out to the fuel companies involved were negligible, the guilty parties were also required to come up with a permanent solution to the run-off problem. This would prove to be a costly undertaking.

The offending companies soon began work to upgrade their oil separation systems and thus reduce and minimize the pollution entering the ditch. However, as the number of trucks using the facilities grew month by month, it became evident that no existing technological system would be able eliminate the fuel wastes.

This is where the story gets interesting.

As you have probably heard, experiments have been done with living organisms that supposedly eat and digest oil products thereby breaking them down and eliminating the danger of pollution. These experiments were started years ago in an attempt to deal with the damage caused by oil tanker spills on the oceans. The companies mentioned earlier had been ordered by the courts to solve the pollution problems that they were obviously causing. Naturally, these same companies wanted to do this as cheaply as possible. So, a hired "environmental specialist" came up with the bright idea of introducing an oil-eating organism to the ditch that had been the cause of all their woes.

I have to admit that at first, whatever they had done seemed to work. I was no longer able to see the usual rainbow sheen on the surface of the ditch whenever it rained. And although the ditch still stank from the oil imbued in its bottom mud, the smell of fresh flowing diesel was no longer to be noticed whenever the rain fell. Yes, things went well ... for a while.

It was encouraging to see ducks and other wildlife return to the ditch's ecosystem. It was truly a pleasure to observe the fish swimming once again among the water plants. The resurgence of these brought back the herons and the kingfishers. Soon, I could hear the frogs do their nightly singing routine as in the past.

One day about a year ago, as I observed the water in the ditch for signs of aquatic life, I noticed a water creature that I had never seen before. It was about the length of a tadpole but it looked like a miniature fat serpent. It was completely black. As I bent down to look closer, I saw several of these creatures swimming about. Suddenly, as I watched, something strange happened. Another of the creatures swam out from among the water plants. It was at least three times the size of the others and before its hapless siblings realized the danger, it had devoured them!

After this incident, I went back several times to see if I could spot one or more of the odd aquatic creatures but I was unable to do so. I did notice however, that the fish started to disappear. And it wasn't just the fish. Little by little, the evening frog choruses grew quieter until before long they became completely silent.   Now, the ducks are gone, the herons and kingfishers have vanished; the area around the ditch has become very still and silent. I am sure that there are fewer birds even.

I have tried several times to alert others to what I think has happened to the "oil-eating organism" experiment but they just laugh at me. I'm thought to be a little eccentric, you see. I have written a few too many letters to the editor in the past. I have made a few too many appearances before the District Council. I'm just another one of those "sh__ disturbers".

Well, that may be. But there have been a few strange happenings around here of late. Why just last week, the neighbour came over accusing me of having done away with his dog. Sure his dog came over here a lot. It even ate some of Miss (that's my female black Labrador)'s dog chow. But that didn't bother me. It was a friendly mutt and a good buddy for

Miss. One thing that I do know for sure is that Miss's friend loved to go for a splash in the ditch. Miss, on the other hand seems paranoid whenever I try to coax her to come anywhere near the watercourse. That's quite strange for a black Labrador.

It gets more interesting. The cops were over here yesterday. They wanted to know if I knew anything about the disappearance of one of the truck stops' employees. Apparently, this fellow stepped out for a cigarette a couple of nights ago and hasn't been seen since. They found his Chicago Bulls cap by an open manhole. Bizarre; weird even...

... It's getting late. It's still raining and the wind is more violent than ever. There goes that noise again. It is definitely something thumping against the sun deck.

Well, spooked or not, I'd better check this out while the deck is still in one piece. I'll finish this later ... if I get the chance...

WHOOSH

ENTER BLOG: 12/01/03 5:47 P.M.

"Whoosh est dans la douche."

It's been a strange day or perhaps it would be better to say a strange couple of hours. I think that I've got a few more minutes before she comes out of the shower so I might as well update my "blog" while this is fresh in my mind. I still have difficulty believing what just happened so perhaps entering it in this on-line journal will allow the late afternoon's happenings to sink in.

I granted my last class at the university an early dismissal, this being the last day in session before the Christmas break. Several students had decided to take make a premature exit anyway so I did not feel very guilty. I gathered up some papers to correct over the holidays and slipped them into my briefcase. I dropped by the faculty lounge to extend my best wishes to some colleagues. I walked out of the modern languages faculty office and headed for the bus stop. There were several buses lined up but, with the university essentially emptying, the bus that I finally managed to get on was very crowded. All the seats were filled and I felt like a kernel in corncob. That's not good for me. I feel uneasy when there are too many people around.

After some moments I noticed that I was sharing the post that I held onto with a woman. She had a knapsack and I assumed she was a student. I am not particularly outgoing but when she smiled, I could not very well ignore her. I smiled back.

She spoke. "You're a professor at the university aren't you?"

"Yes, I am actually," I replied. "How did you know?"

"Well, you are aren't you?" And she smiled a mysterious smile not unlike that of the Mona Lisa's which has perplexed so many for so long. Why did I think of the Mona Lisa? She did not look at all like her. I felt nervous. I am really not one to make small talk with strangers but something about her, and I have to admit I don't know what, made me want her to go on with the conversation.

"What's your name?" she demanded.

Taken aback with this forward approach with which I am completely unfamiliar, I stammered a bit but answered, "Gerald. Gerald Audray. Most people call me Ger."

"Audray," she said. "That's French isn't it?"

"Yes," I replied. "My parents were from France actually."

"I know that," she said. "My name is Whoosh."

I tried not to show my reaction but I really was beginning to think at this point that she was having me on. I almost started to panic. I cannot stand the thought of being me a fool of particularly not by a woman for whom I was beginning to develop some early feelings of attraction and women easily intimidate me without even knowing they're doing it.

"That's an original name," I said. "Whoosh who?"

"Just Whoosh," she replied.

I smiled stupidly not knowing what else to say. I was still trying to figure out if she was being serious. Her facial expressions did not give much away. She did not strike me as a beautiful woman in the sense of a fashion model or a movie star but she was most definitely very attractive in the way she came across; she exuded an aura of innocence and yet quite the opposite at the same time. There was an undeniable essence about her which was almost palpable.

My stop came and went. I thought that I would stay on until she got off and take another bus or a cab back to my place. She began asking me all sorts of questions and I continued to feel more than a bit silly because she seemed to know the answers before I gave them. I don't know how many times she said "I know."

The bus arrived downtown at the end of the line. Now I truly felt like a fool.

"You don't live around here do you?" she asked.

"No. I missed my stop. I live in Killarney Heights actually. What about you? You live around here?"

"No. I was hoping you would tell me where I should stay."

Well, what could I say? The whole event was too unusually unlike my daily routine. So without thinking, which is most unlike me, I took a chance.

I did not know what to say so I said something like this.

"Okay... ...so. All right then. "Well, if you have no place to stay, you're welcome in my home." I couldn't believe I'd actually said that but she gave me no time to ponder that and she did not appear at all surprised.

"I accept with pleasure and I am grateful," she replied.

We took a cab to my place and she asked if she could use the shower...

...Oh, I think she's just about done because she has stopped singing. She's got an enchanting voice but I can't recognize any of her songs.

Here she comes. Wow...!?!

"Whoosh est sortie de la douche."

EXIT BLOG: 12/01/03 6:11 P.M.

THE LEGEND OF FAWCETT BROOK

The story goes like this: Once upon a time, no one can say exactly when, there lived on the mountain called "Chilliwack" a young maiden who lives there still, although most folks have never seen her. At the time in question, she went by the name of Brooke Fawcett. She lived with her father a fair way up the mountain, deep in the forest.

Brooke was a beautiful young woman. She had dark blue eyes and long, lustrous black hair that reflected even the most distant starlight on moonless nights. Brooke was lithe and agile because of her daily duty of herding the sheep to the few meadows that she could find amidst the deep forest of the mountain.

Brooke lived alone with her father. Her mother, Leah, had died giving birth to Brooke. Her father told her many things about her mother. Although he was sad when his wife had died, he had been prepared for it. Leah had told him that, when her first child was born, she would be leaving to go back to her people. She did not say where this was, but Brooke's father felt that it was a good place. He also told Brooke about Leah's special powers and that these had been passed on to her from her mother when she had gone on with her journey.

As a certain sign of these powers, Leah had left a staff for her daughter and Brooke never went anywhere without it. Brooke loved her life on the mountain. After her father left to work in the village in the valley far below, Brooke would herd the sheep to a meadow and watch over them until the sun was low in the west over the mighty river that flowed to the distant sea.

Brooke did not have any people friends. She seldom went to the village, only visiting there when someone who had taken ill summoned her through her father. As in all human communities from all time, there were some in the village who, through fear of mystery and what they could not understand, thought that Brooke was a witch. They said that she got her powers from the devil. So, although Brooke never refused to go to the village to heal someone who believed in her, she preferred to stay in the forest on the mountain. For there, she had no lack of friends. She could talk with the birds and the animals and indeed, they would often gather around her without fear. As well, Brooke could often hear her mother's words of love and encouragement in the sigh of the wind and in the rustle of the leaves. And she would often see her mother smiling at her from some cloud sailing slowly by.

Yes, Brooke truly loved her life and she would not have exchanged it with anyone in the world. The climate where Brooke and her father lived was ideal. It did not matter the season, it was never too hot nor ever too cold. Even when people in the village complained about the harshness of the weather at times, Brooke and her father never found reason to agree with them.

One fateful day in the fall however, a sudden, unexpected storm came over the mountains along the great river from the north. Brooke had felt something in the air since she had awakened that morning; but, as was her duty, she led the sheep to a distant meadow so that they could graze on what was left of the grass.

The storm was savage. The wind blew suddenly in freezing gusts and a heavy snow started to fall. In a very short time, it was very hard to see through the blowing snow. Brooke began to herd the sheep back home. The ground was slippery and suddenly, one of the smallest lambs disappeared down a dark hollow in the ground. Through the howling wind, Brooke could hear its plaintive bleats. She followed the sounds and soon located the unfortunate creature. She could not leave it behind. She laid her staff on the ground, now covered with snow, and reached to pull the lamb to safety.

Just as she managed to do so, the staff started to slide down the mountainside. In an instant, it had vanished in the swirling snowflakes and the darkness beneath the giant trees. Brooke was struck with panic but she would not let the sheep freeze to their death. She herded them to the safety and warmth of their shelter. Once she had made sure that they were all accounted for, she fed them hay and bid them a good night.

Her duty done, Brooke immediately went back into the storm to search for her precious staff. She looked and she looked until her eyes became dim. The storm grew in violence. It was as if all the evil spirits had descended upon the mountain. Brooke began to feel weak. She could no longer feel her limbs. She was freezing. Finally, well after darkness had fallen and still the wind and snow did not abate, she saw the staff. Its slide had been halted by a giant cedar. Brooke bent down to reach for it, and fell in the snow. As she touched the beloved link to her mother, she smiled but she did not get back up.

In the spring of the following year, as Brooke's father herded the sheep towards a meadow, he heard something that caught his attention because it was most unusual. It was like a girl's laughter. It seemed to come from the direction of a very large cedar tree. Curious, he followed the sounds. A few strides brought him to a sight that stirred his deepest emotions. Next to his daughter's staff, a spring bubbled out of the ground and tumbled over large rocks towards the mighty river below. He was suddenly overcome with an incredible sense of relief and of joy. He felt the presence of both Leah, his beloved wife, and of his cherished daughter, Brooke. As he watched the water flowing from the earth, his eyes filled with tears and he closed them for an instant. When he opened them again, the staff had vanished.

That is the legend of Brooke Fawcett. If you visit Chilliwack Mountain, you can find evidence that this legend is true. Along one of the many roads that wind through the forests of the mountain, there is a brook that is marked on the maps of the region. It is called Fawcett Brook. If you find it, as I have been fortunate enough to have done, you will hear a maiden laughing and your heart will have wings.

THE STRANGER

...Hey, Doc! Up here on the deck. I hope you didn't have a hard time finding the place. Set back from the road as it is and with the trees and all, it's easy to think you're going to get lost eh? Here, have a seat. What a beautiful evening! I'd just as soon we sat out here if you don't mind. The house gets kind of hot after a day such as we've had. Oh, I see you've brought a bottle. Whoever told you a little wine loosens my tongue and puts me in a better disposition; well, I admit I do like a glass of wine or two now and then. Not the way I used to, you understand...

...I learned my lesson the hard way, if you know what I mean. I fell down pretty hard. But I got up again. I've got a feeling that what you're here for will connect to that part of my life as well. That'll be for you to figure out though. I mean, you're the expert, right? You're the one with the fancy degree and I guess that entitles you to do your research, to ask your questions and to get paid handsomely for it. Sorry if I sound a little sarcastic, Doc. It's just that I don't hold much to you fancy guys with your suits and ties and your fancy cars. Hey, don't take it personal, you could prove me wrong. By the way, Doc; let me tell you right off. I'm a former teacher who prefers to express himself in layman's terms. Sometimes though, I forget which level of language to use. If this happens this evening, I hope you'll forgive me. I'm not as young as I used to be and I don't care much about making impressions anymore...

...Thanks, Doc. That is good wine. It's a lot better than what I can afford...

...Yeah, yeah, I'll get to that in due time...

... Would you look at those stars? ... Magnificent, don't you think? Looking at that expanse always makes me feel so insignificant and yet, a part of it all. You know, when the wind is from the east as it is tonight, it drives away the city's filth from the sky and it brings the smell of evergreens from those mountains over there. It's one of my greatest pleasures, Doc; to sit here and take it all in. Sometimes I even fall asleep and wake up when it gets too cold. It's a bonus this time of year to have the frogs croaking up a storm. You know, if I could find the leader of that chorus, I'd give him or her an award. Just think, to sing like that hour after hour and still have time to keep the mosquitoes under control. That's something isn't it...?

...You're an impatient man, Doc. What are you in such a hurry for anyway? In a little while, you're going to get back in your flashy machine and race back to the city. Sit back and enjoy this for a while. It might do you some good. You seem more than a little uptight. Relax, Doc. I'll tell you what you want to hear. But I'll do it when I'm ready; in the right frame of mind, if you hear what I'm saying...

...So you don't believe much in unsolved mysteries or psychic phenomena, Doc? Well, I never used to either. I mean, as far as I was concerned, people who believe in flying saucers and ghosts and such had just about as much credibility with me as a politician running for re-election. But I've changed my mind about a lot of things, Doc. I think that you'll come to see why as we wear out this evening and put this fine wine to good use. Yeah, I'll tell you the story you came to hear. All I ask is that you try to keep an open mind. Ask yourself what I have to gain by telling you a pack of fancy lies. Even though I'm sure I'm not as busy as you, Doc; I've got better things to do with my time than to spend the hours dreaming up complicated stories just for the entertainment of fancy fellows like yourself...

...Thanks. Mmm, that is indeed very good. Well, here goes...

...The first time that I saw her, I was walking in those woods over there. It was a couple of years ago though it seems longer than that in some ways. It's almost impossible to put a time to it. It's hard to explain, but trying to put a time frame on it seems to cheapen the experience. I don't know if you can understand what I'm trying to get across to you...

...Anyway, as I was saying, the first time I saw her; it was one of those incredibly lovely days in early spring. The air was intoxicating with the smell of rebirth and renewed growth, wild Easter lilies had just begun blooming and the moss was soft, like an emerald carpet on the forest floor. The birds were excited about the new season and they kept telling each other about it...

...I had just come upon the clearing where the lilies are the most abundant when I heard the sound of singing. At first it sounded like wind chimes accompanying a soft female voice. Then it was like a whisper on the wind passing through the branches of the trees above my head. I looked in the direction of the sound and there she was, sitting on a fallen tree...

...When I saw her, Doc; I had the most incredible sense of déjà vu that I've ever experienced. It was like a dream. As a matter of fact, it **was** exactly like a dream that I'd had a few times before. You've heard of love at first sight, Doc; well this was it for me. But I don't want you to get the wrong idea. I mean, she was beautiful, very attractive and all. But she wasn't glowing and wearing flimsy flowing gowns or anything like that. She was dressed pretty much the way someone going for a walk in the woods would be dressed...

...What I'm trying to say is that the attraction that I felt for her was much more than physical. Again, it's hard to put in plain words. It felt as if I were dreaming and feeling the way you do in dreams and when you wake up; you want to keep that feeling going but you can't and you feel cheated and sad. But this time, the feeling was there and it wasn't going away. I knew it was coming from her. She had this incredible aura of confident peace and joy about her. I must have looked awfully stupid with my mouth open and gaping at her. But I didn't feel stupid. When she finally spoke, Doc; it was natural. I felt as though I'd known her for a long, long time. I could speak to her more easily than I've ever been able to speak to even my closest family members and friends...

...Thanks, Doc...

...Well, we came back here and she stayed with me for about a month. She taught me a lot, Doc. Mostly she taught me about myself and how I fit in. She never did come right out and tell me where she came from but she did imply that I could figure it out for myself if I really wanted to. She never told me her name. She said that names weren't important at this particular time. So I gave her one. I called her Roxanne after the young woman in the story about that long-nosed Cyrano de Bergerac guy. I had seen the movie and I really liked the lady poor Cyrano was in love with, although he was too weak-kneed to tell her. She seemed so innocent and pure and perfect, like an angel, if that's what angels are supposed to be like. So I named my visitor after her. Roxanne didn't mind. And you know, she wasn't so high and mighty either that she wouldn't stoop to do some housework and chores...

...I don't want you getting the wrong idea though, Doc. Our relationship was purely platonic as they say. I was attracted to her; I mean, who wouldn't have been? She's beautiful. But this inexplicable sensation that surrounded her seemed above the physical things around us. It's hard to explain this as I've said before. I guess you had to be there. All I can say is that the time she spent here was wonderful in a way that can't be put into words very easily...

...I think that even if I managed to explain what I mean, it would never do justice to the way it felt being with her. But finally, she must have become tired of giving the wagging tongues in town something to wag about. Maybe she thought that I was ready to try life on my own. I don't really know; but one day, I came back from work and she was gone. She didn't leave a note or anything but I knew it was time; it felt sad but right somehow. You'd think I would have been all melancholy and teary-eyed and full of despair, wouldn't you? Well, I admit that sometimes I do miss her physical presence. But Doc, believe it or not; Roxanne has never left. I feel her presence all the time even if I don't actually see her. Oh, and the dreams I have, Doc. If I could put them on the screen, I do believe there'd be a lot of happier people about...

...The story doesn't end here, Doc. I'm sure that you've heard of others around here that've had a strange experience or two with an unknown stranger from God-knows-where. Well, just because I'm the only one willing to tell the story doesn't mean that it didn't happen. More than one person has been on this deck to share their experience with me. More than one person from this two-bit town has been here because they know that I won't laugh at them.

And Doc, they've told me about a wonderful stranger that changed **their** lives. Some have called the stranger

"Cindy", "Helen", "Venus", and even "Gabriel". I could tell you the stories that they have shared with me but that wouldn't be fair. If they wanted you to know, they would have agreed to see you. Maybe someday they will want to make their experiences public and that would make for another fine evening, Doc. I can share a couple of things that I've observed though, if you don't mind staying just a tad longer and sharing a little more of that fancy wine...

...Thank you, Doc. That does help to keep the night's clammy hands back for a bit longer, doesn't it...?

...You see, Doc; there have been changes in the lives of some people around here. You take that young couple, Bobby and Nikki Dobson. They got married a year ago mostly because they had to. Four months after, they had this little one. I can tell you, Doc; in this town, you had better be married for better or for worse if you're going to shack up and have a child. That's the way it's always been around here. If you don't like it, you'd better be prepared to pack up and find another town to live in because people around here can make life pretty miserable for what they call a bastard child...

...Anyway, Bobby and Nikki were married for better or for worse, mostly for worse as it turned out. Bobby worked on and off; mostly off. Then he took to drinking to drown his problems, I guess. Well, luckily for Nikki, Bobby isn't the violent type when he's been drinking. Mostly he gets emotional for a bit and then falls asleep. But Nikki, she's got spunk and she wouldn't sit there and watch her husband destroy himself without letting him and the neighbours know what she thinks of it. So it was that for all these months, everybody knew when Bobby had had a few too many. Nikki wasn't shy about letting him and the other tenants within earshot know how she felt about it all. They were about to be evicted from their place when, incredibly, their problems seemed to disappear. Bobby still has trouble finding steady work but Nikki's complaints have stopped...

...Why, just this morning, I saw them and the little girl in the park. The little girl was on one of the red swings, swinging in the blue sky, laughing with the swallows flitting around her; and her mom and dad were holding hands and smiling their love at her. Quite a change isn't it, Doc? Hard to explain...

...I know that as much as Nikki and Bobby may have wanted to go to marriage counselling, they couldn't afford it. But I'll tell you something, Doc. There's been counselling and mending and loving going on. I'll let you stew about who I think might have been involved. And no, Doc; I'm not going to tell you whether or not Bobby or Nikki or even that sweet little girl of theirs has breathed a word of what happened in their lives and how it came about. I can tell you this though: there was a stranger who rented an apartment not too long ago in the complex where that young, struggling family lives...

...You make of it what you will, Doc. Maybe that fancy degree of yours will help you figure it out although I kind of doubt it. Sorry, Doc. Here I go again being rude and ornery. It's just that my experience with fancy fellows has been rather disappointing over the years. And that's putting it in a nice way...

...Have you had enough, Doc? Not too cold are you? I love it out here. Smell the mountain scents carried along on the night breeze. Listen to those frogs, man. Doesn't it make you glad that you can still hear that in this time we're going through? That's a great horned owl you're hearing, Doc. Look at those stars. Makes us seem kind of small don't it, Doc? I mean, we're just another one of those little flecks on the canvas of the universe aren't we? Not much bigger than a fly speck really. Just another dust mote floating about in endless space with an unknown destination. Makes me feel small yet important somehow; important and grateful to be a part of it all. What do you think, Doc...?

...If you want and if you're willing to part with another drop or two of your fancy wine, I can tell you another little anecdote about our town that might give you something to chew over on your way back to the big city. What do you say, Doc...?

...Thank you, my good man. Sorry, I'm getting a little too condescending. But you know, Doc; I really do get the feeling that you're a lot more interested in this than you were at first. I'm encouraged by that. I think that there might be hope for you. Ah, I'm sorry! There I go again. I am incorrigible. My wife used to say that about me. I cannot resist poking a little fun where poking is needed. But you'll admit Doc, I do poke gently...

...I'll share one more story with you and then we'll call it a night, Doc. This one concerns one young lady in this town who was an indisputable bitch (pardon the language, Doc, but it is as good a way as any to describe this person to you in the least number of words possible). I don't want you to get the idea that this young woman got to be that way on her own accord. Her father was an abuser of the worst kind. Her mother abandoned her when she was three years old. She had to learn to cope and she did by becoming what I have already said she was...

...Belinda McPhail could take care of herself. In the second grade, she gave the class bully a profusely bleeding nose when he took exception to her size and decided to make it an opportunity for laughter at her expense. He never did this again and his bullying days were over. There was a new bully at the school and her name was Belinda "Bubba" McPhail. I'm simply sharing these few details, Doc, so that you can see for yourself that Ms. McPhail was not someone to make fun of to her face...

...When she was fourteen years old, she got tired of her drunken father's advances and bashed him over the head with his bowling ball. The town was well rid of Mr. McPhail as was his daughter. It did mean however, that Belinda would finish her growing up being transferred from one foster home to another...

...Later on, Belinda became one of the town's few taxi drivers and I can tell you Doc, that no one has ever bragged about stiffing her for the fare. In fact, it is common knowledge that Belinda gets the largest tips from her customers. If you meet Belinda, Doc, you'll know that she probably does not get her tips from her looks or her general disposition; at least, not until recently. But you know, Doc? Can you guess who I saw holding hands with James Hannigan at the lake last Sunday afternoon? You've guessed it, Doc. Yes indeed...!

...There was Belinda "Bubba" McPhail walking hand in hand and chatting happily with the town head librarian, one Mr. James Hannigan. Mr. Hannigan, Doc, is lucky if he weighs one half as much as does his recently acquired girlfriend. I'll tell you something else, Doc. James has been the butt of a lot of jokes in this town since he was a kid because of his love of art and books and such. But the look on their faces, Doc. Those two are in love. And you know what, Doc? No one is laughing. That's strange for a town like this. Two years ago, those two would have been a laughingstock, behind Belinda's back of course because you wouldn't have wanted to look at her the wrong way if you cared for the current contours of your face...

...And I'll tell you yet one more thing about this wonderful development, Doc. Belinda McPhail and James Hannigan both rent an apartment in the same complex as does the young Dobson couple. What do you make of that, Doc? Coincidence? Fate? Luck? Maybe, Doc. If you think that Roxanne, or Venus, or Gabriel or whoever he or she is, is just that; it's up to you, Doc. You can think what you like. As long as you're thinking and as long as you're doing what I asked you to do earlier: to keep an open mind...

...I'm getting tired, Doc; and it is getting a little chilly out here. You've probably got a full day's work tomorrow so you'll be wanting to get back. I'm pretty well finished telling you what you came to hear anyway. I've just told you the obvious, the easily understood. If I went into what Roxanne began to teach me about everything, we would still be here tomorrow night and probably the night after that...

...I don't want you to think that I believe I've got it all figured out. Roxanne has opened the door to another way, to another dimension perhaps. I am not more intelligent than you Doc, but I sense that I've told you enough. If you want to know more, it's up to you. Roxanne is not mine nor Bobby's nor Belinda's nor the Dobsons'. I think you can understand that he or she is one of many or perhaps one of many of one. I am not sure. It seems unimportant somehow. What is important is that you and I understand that we are here to learn. This is our learning place, our school, if you will. Some of us are slow learners. We keep being put back. We will keep being put back until we learn. That is why that old saying makes sense, Doc. You know, the one about the more things change, the more they stay the same. It seems that systems and leaders in these systems keep making the same mistakes. They are slow learners, Doc. Those who have learned have moved on. They have gone home...

...Thanks for coming by Doc, and thank you for the wine. Watch your step. The stairs can be slippery at night. Drive carefully and keep an open mind, Doc. I'll be here if you want to talk some more sometime but you might be better off trying to contact your own angel. We've all got at least one who's willing to help us out, you know; that is, if we allow it. Well, so long, Doc...

THE LITTLE PEOPLE

Once upon a time in a deep and green valley far away from here, there lived some little people who had come upon a problem.

The little people had a leader whose name was Tipop (pronounced **[tee-pop]**). The problem had come about as the result of Tipop's daughter who had come of age and whose time had come to marry.

Tradition as well as the law of the land decreed that once the leader's daughter had to find a husband, it was necessary to climb out of the lovely valley, to go over the mountains and to summon a young man from a village on the other side.

So it was that Tina (pronounced **[tee-nah]**), the village leader's daughter, was now waiting for the likely young man whom she would wed. Before this could happen however, it was necessary for a messenger to be sent to the village on the other side of the mountains.

Unfortunately, it had been a very long time since a messenger had been sent forth to summon a suitor for the village leader's daughter. So it had come about that no one could remember the best way to achieve this.

The village leader, Tipop, called a meeting of all the able young men of the village and asked for volunteers to act as messenger. Many young men came forth eager to offer their help.

The first to be chosen for the task was Timac (pronounced **[tee-mack]**) for he was the eldest of the young men of the village and he had a map of the path that crossed the mountains. Timac set forth from the village early one morning. He walked through the forest, climbing higher and higher up in the mountains that separated his village from the one he sought. At first, he made good progress. He listened to the birds that sang, he inhaled the fresh mountain air, and he sang and whistled as he climbed. After several hours of climbing, Timac encountered snow. The more he went up, the deeper the snow became. Soon Timac was unable to go further. The snow was too deep and he could not continue. Discouraged, Timac turned back down the mountain and returned to his village.

No one in the village blamed Timac for his failed attempt. Tipop called another meeting and it was then that Timan (pronounced **[tee-man]**) reminded everyone that he had a pair of snowshoes that would enable him to walk over the snow. This gave new hope to everyone and so it was that Timan was chosen to be the messenger who would call forth Tina's husband.

Timan set off immediately. Soon he was in the deep snow. He had no difficulty walking over the deep drifts for his snowshoes enabled him to walk without sinking. However, before long, darkness fell and Timan could not see where he was going. Disappointed, he turned around and soon was back in the village. Although he had failed in his mission, no one blamed him for he had done his best.

It was time for another meeting. Tipop called the villagers together. This time, another young man, one by the name of Tidude (pronounced **[tee-doode]**), informed everyone that he had a lantern that would light his way in the dark. Everyone agreed that he should be the next to try to make his way to the village across the mountains.

Tidude left without delay and soon he was high in the mountains. Darkness fell but it caused no worry for Tidude as his lantern showed him the way. Unfortunately, just as he was about to cross the highest peak, a wicked storm descended upon the mountains. The wind blew cold and hard, the snow fell, and Tidude began to feel very numb. It was not long before he felt himself begin to freeze. It was no use. Tidude realized that it was best to turn around. Soon, he was back in his village; safe but sad.

Tipop and the people of the village were getting desperate. Another meeting was called. This time, another eager young man volunteered. It was Tiluc (pronounced **[tee-luke]**). He pointed out that he had a warm winter coat which no wind could ever get through. All of the villagers cheered as he set out to cross the mountains.

Tiluc made good progress. At first, he did not wear his winter coat because he would have been too warm. Instead, he carried it on his back. However, as he climbed higher and higher and the cold, stormy wind began to chill him, he put on his coat. Tiluc laughed at the stormy wind. He felt warm inside his coat. He truly felt that he would soon reach his destination.

Not long after crossing the highest peak, Tiluc began to feel very hungry. He was determined so he kept on walking. After some time however, he began to feel weak, and just as he looked far away, down in the valley at the village where he was meant to take his message, Tiluc fell from exhaustion. He understood that he was unable to continue. So it was that soon he was back in his village. He too had failed.

Tipop and the villagers were truly despairing now. No one knew what to do. Each felt that somehow, they had forgotten a very important rule but no one could say what that rule was.

It was then that Tina, whom all the fuss was about, came forward. She asked for Timac, Timan, Tidude and Tiluc to gather around her. She asked them if each would be willing to lend her his special possession. The four young men eagerly agreed even though each secretly thought that Tina would never succeed in her quest. From Timac, she obtained the map which showed the way across the mountains. From Timan, she got the precious snowshoes which would allow her to walk on the snow. Tidude happily let her have his lantern. Tina then asked Tiluc for his warm coat and he graciously agreed to lend it to her.

It was time for Tina to leave. Her father asked: "What will you eat, my daughter? You know how Tiluc grew weak from hunger."

"Have you forgotten Nana (pronounced **[nah-nah]**), my faithful goat, father?" replied Tina. "With her milk, the map, the snowshoes, the lantern, and the coat, I will find my way to the village on the other side of the mountains."

So it came about that not long afterwards, there was a feast in the village of the lovely, green valley of the little people. Tina had found a most suitable husband and he felt that Tina was as wise and wonderful a wife as he could ever wish for.

As the years went by and Tina and her husband raised their children, they taught them the lesson that the villagers had relearned through Tina: When people work together, a solution to a problem, whatever it may be, can surely be found. Cooperation does indeed work wonders

NIGHTMARE AT THE MALL

I hate shopping malls. When I need something from the store, I like to go in, choose the item, pay for it and get out. However, with two daughters recently having reached their teens, I must admit that I frequent shopping establishments quite a lot more than I would like.

Take today, for example. The kids are on spring break as am I, being a teacher in a local high school. The girls had me promise in a moment of weakness that I would take them shopping at least once during the holidays. Well, here we are. My son Marc decided that he would tag along and I am glad for the company.

For what seems like hours, we have been going from store to store as the girls check things out. Marc and I follow along going from bench to bench (and I am thankful for those provided). It seems like the fiftieth time that we have sat down and watched the girls go into yet another boutique. This latest one has an attractive neon logo. It vibrates its name, "The Exotique," as the music from within bops and booms.

I settle down on the bench just outside the entrance to the latest of the girls' hunting grounds. Marc is leafing through a magazine, probably checking the latest on computer news or recent developments regarding Star Trek.

Well, I might as well relax and do what I like the most in a less than desirable situation: people watch. I find it fascinating to look at individuals going by and picturing what their lives must be like. With the majority of the young crowd, it is hard to be creatively imaginative since they all seem to fit into some fairly narrow categories: skaters, rappers, jocks, preppies or rockers. However, when one observes those who have reached the age of having to make ends meet, it is quite different. The variety is endless and most interesting. I look and envision, watch and imagine, observe and think, see and absorb…

…My eyes return to The Exotique. Its full glass frontal facade allows for a good view of the front of the store. Something begins to bother me. I see people going into the shop but I realize that I have yet to see anyone come out. And, where are the girls? I glance at my watch. What? That can't be! We've been outside this joint for over an hour? The girls rarely spend more than fifteen minutes in any one location and, if they do, I can count on Marc to go in and remind them that we are waiting. I glance at Marc. He seems absorbed in some article in his magazine.

"Marc, would you go and see if the girls are ready to come out of there? They've been in there for over an hour!"

"Sure, Dad," and off he goes.

I watch as he disappears among racks of the latest fashions. I wait. I look around. Something seems to have gone wrong with the lighting around me. I glance back at The Exotique. It looks darker in there, somehow not quite right. Shoppers keep filtering in but still, no one is coming out. I am getting a strange feeling of foreboding in the pit of my consciousness. What's going on? Where's Marc? Where are the girls? I'm sure the interior of The Exotique is getting darker. I've got to check this out but I'll be a mall lover before I walk in there. I yell out at one of the salespersons, "Hey, you! What's going on in there?

"What do you mean, sir," responds a handsome, well-dressed young man.

"Look, my kids have been in this shop for well over an hour and I'm tired of waiting. I want them out here now!"

"Why, sir, we do not force anyone to stay in our establishment against their will. I'm sure your children will come out when they have finished doing business with us." He nods with a smug smile.

He continues, "Why don't you come in yourself, sir. I'm sure you can find something that would interest you among our incredible variety of styles and real offerings; if you know what I mean." He actually winks. Now I am really getting unnerved.

"Look, I am not in the least bit interested in your fancy clothes. I want my kids out of your outfit and I want them back with me now!"

"There's no need to get upset, sir; and please do keep your voice down. I would not like to have to call for security and make an unpleasant scene out of this." He gives me that self-assured grin of his once again. I have this almost uncontrollable urge to punch him or to yank his fancy tie once or twice; but I'm not that kind of guy.

He goes on, "Why don't you come on in and have a look around, sir. I am certain that you will quickly realize why your children have been so captivated by our wares."

"Go to hell! I wouldn't step in your two-bit outfit if you promised me a free shopping spree. I've been watching this place of yours. Why is it that a good number of people go in your joint but no one ever comes out, hey? Explain that, smiley!"

"Ah, my good man, you have stumbled upon the secret of our fine establishment. We are the only shop in the mall to have two accesses. Our customers come in through this entry here before you and they leave by the one at the rear of our premises. You see, my fine sir, "The Exotique" is quite unique. Oh, and by the way, sir, your daughters are most attractive." He laughs a most irritating and somewhat challenging laugh.

"Are you telling me that my kids have left your shop through the back? That makes no sense. They know where I'm waiting."

"Oh, my fine gentleman, I have not stated that your children have left us but we do encourage our customers to leave through the back entry."

"Why?" I scream in frustration.

"It is simply in their best interests to do so. You really should come in, though. I believe that I just saw your children trying on some of our finer garments in those fitting rooms over there."

Reluctantly, I have to admit to myself that he is right. If my kids are in the shop, I don't want them leaving it through the other entrance where I will surely lose contact with them. I seem to lose my sense of direction in these places.

I step into the shop. Something is definitely wrong here. The music is like none that I'd ever heard before. The light is wrong. I can't quite make out where I'm going. Suddenly, I'm falling down, down, down into complete darkness. It's like dropping down a well. As I fall, I can hear the young salesman laughing eerily, "Bon voyage, sir, ha! ha! ha!..."

... "Sir? Sir? Are you all right?"

I'm lying on the bench looking up into the concerned face of the young salesman.

"What? Yes, yes I'm fine. I guess I must have dozed off or something. Sorry about that."

"No problem, sir."

It doesn't take long for reality to set in.

"That was so-o-o-o embarrassing, Dad!" exclaims my daughter Jo as we leave the vicinity of The Exotique.

"Embarrassing for you, sweetie; terrifying for me. I'm just glad you're still here," and I give her a hug.

She gives me a smile and a questioning look as her sister Crystal exclaims, "Jo, look; it's Off The Wall!"

I look for Marc. He's already found another bench.

Whew... ...I need to get a good night's sleep.

THE INCIDENT

(some adult language)

Doctor Ryan Thorpe stepped out of the black sedan and walked directly towards the young man standing a few meters away. Thorpe's appearance gave the impression of a man who is very sure of himself, a man obviously accustomed to getting results.

"You simply must tell me about this incident in the forest, Mr. Newman. My organization is being pressed for answers from the authorities and we cannot be patient any longer. Now, if I am to understand, you and some friends were out there having a party."

"Now just you wait a second!" interrupted Tim Newman.

He was a young man who could not have been much more than twenty years of age. He was slight of build and rather handsome with his dark complexion although he gave the impression of being somewhat distraught while trying not to show it.

He went on, "That's a real good one. You and your so-called associates or whatever the hell you call them, are getting impatient. Well, I really feel for you all. What about me, hey? This is the third time in five days that you've come here uninvited. I told the cops and I told the press and I'm telling you one more time; I have absolutely no intention of talking about what happened in those woods. Get that through your head full of PhD bullshit and get the hell out of here!"

"I don't think you understand, Mr. Newman. We simply must get at the truth. Three young people from this community vanished that night. We have been kind enough to give you a break to get over the shock, that's all." Thorpe wearily glanced towards the distant forest. "You were with them. You're the only one who can help us get at the truth. And, of course, we can help you."

Newman laughed sarcastically. "The truth. Yeah, sure. You and your boys, whoever you really are, you have so much truth from incidents, as you call them, from the past fifty years, you can't keep it from starting to leak out all over the place. Who are you working for anyway? As if I need to ask! Is it the military, the CIA, the FBI, the National Enquirer; or maybe all of the above? Each one of them has about the same degree of credibility. What a joke! Even if I were to tell you what happened, which I cannot do, you'd somehow twist it all around; make me look like some kind of local idiot psycho and move on to control the next incident. No thanks, man, just forget it. I know damn well I'll be better off without your kind of help.

Thorpe tried to appear more menacing and the tone of his voice indicated his rising frustration as he continued, "You are going to force our hand and I can assure you, Mr. Newman, you will not come out of this the winner. There is too much power bearing down upon you. You cannot stop the system. There are rules here and procedures to be followed. The security of the nation could be at stake here. People panic so easily, Mr. Newman. You have no choice but to co-operate with us if you ever hope to resume some kind of normal life."

The young Newman looked visibly angered by the last of the doctor's statement. He raised his voice considerably and there was a noticeable twitch of his left cheek as he exclaimed, "I told you to go to hell and I meant it! If you think you can just come over here whenever you choose and threaten me, you obviously haven't done a very good job of studying my latest psychological profile; or maybe it's just not in the files yet, hey? Is that it? Well, I don't give a damn. You talked about patience earlier. Guess what, I just ran out of it.

I've got work to do, doc; work of a higher order you might say, and the guys and gals I work for don't give any breaks. They don't give a shit about my state of shock because they're experts at giving it. Now, I'll give you ten seconds to walk back to that shiny black boat of yours and scram!

"You know very well that I cannot do that, Newman. I will go back to the car. Oh yes indeed. I will place a call for assistance and that, my young obstinate, misguided friend, will be the end of your little charade. Never say that I did not give you a chance."

He turned and walked away but he would have thought twice about it had he seen the look on Newman's face. The latter's eyes seemed about ready to explode from his head. His face had become very pale and contorted and he was in obvious pain. Suddenly, before Thorpe had taken a mere three steps, the younger man leaped into the air with superhuman agility and strength. Before the unfortunate Doctor Thorpe realized what was happening, he lay on the ground with Newman's hands at his throat. The doctor had little time to marvel at the strength in the slight young man's hands before he blacked out into unconsciousness.

Newman got up. He seemed to have regained some of his former control. He looked down at the inert Thorpe and shook his head.

"It's not like I didn't give you a chance, doc." He chuckled softly. "I just hope you're not afraid of ants because you're about to meet some pretty big and very advanced ones. And man, can they fly! If you ever liked Star Trek, you are going to love this. Sure, there'll be a little pain at first, but you get used to it."

For a moment, Newman seemed to freeze on the spot as he turned his gaze towards the sky. A sudden thick shaft of very bright light surrounded the two men as their silhouettes blurred. A moment later, they had vanished. Only the large black sedan with its official plates remained in the otherwise nondescript yard.

PART TWO – WHISPERS

Some thoughts from Régis...

"There is no halting time since it is forever; this moment is eternity if one wishes it to be so."

"Life has its inevitable tears but our laughter and our love transform them into precious pearls."

"One should find happiness within oneself. That is like finding the pot of gold at the end of the proverbial rainbow. But first, one must find the rainbow."

"Sadly, most of us are so overwhelmed by the 'busy-ness' of living that we do not take time to truly live and enjoy the gift of life given to us."

"It does not matter where one lives; neither how lovely nor ugly the place; it is the dwelling in one's heart that truly matters."

"Does one ever run out of tears, and if so, what happens then?"

"The serenity of a slowly flowing stream caresses the senses."

"Be wary of promises made during the ecstasy of passion."

"Were I able to compose an aria of your holistic beauty, it would be sought after by the most famous of opera singers."

"Passion blinds reason."

"Each relationship, be it a romance or a friendship, is unique and like a snowflake, can be fragile. It is beautiful and to be treasured and taken care of, lest it melt away and all that is left is a tear."

"There is no healing without forgiveness."

"The winds of fanaticism stir the sands of hatred and spread conflict throughout the land; and no oasis of peace will be found until all accept one another as one."

"The earth breathes... ...and grows trees."

"What a joy to lie down in the shade of your loveliness!"

"Before one can truly appreciate "paradise" in this world, one has to find it first within oneself."

"Although it is said that patience is a virtue, it can be lonely."

"Your love is my preferred melody as it pleasantly plays in my heart."

"You came into my life when I was on the edge of hell and opened the door to heaven."

"The seed of friendship must be planted and nurtured so that love may grow."

"Love is the best lubricant for smoothly gliding blissfully through life."

"Should you decide to cease playing the music of your love to which you have introduced me, I really do not know if I could learn to sing again."

"It is more than extraordinarily sad that, in such an overpopulated world, the dismal knell of loneliness is echoing in so many souls."

"If I were a stone and you were a stream, I would love the sense of your being flowing all around and over me and perhaps even through me."

"The symphony of life would be incomplete without the celestial music of your love."

"Love is the delectable cherry on my heavenly Sundae... ...Mondae, Tuesdae, Wednesdae, Thursdae, Fridae, Saturdae."

"My armour may be somewhat dented and dulled in places but I am still your knight and you are nonetheless my lady if you will."

"As long as men persist in making war instead of music, poetry, and love; peace will not be freed from her shackles."

"Love is a treasure that can neither be bought nor sold. It is sad that, due to warped perceptions, some are afraid to give love away while others fear to receive it."

"I would be delighted to walk with you in the moonlight, in the mystical loveliness of a summer's night."

"In the dimness of the depth of night, uncertainty and unease stir in my soul but they are kept at bay by the vigilant light of your love."

"As the moon slowly sails behind a copse of clouds, there is a whisper of wind, and I think of you."

"The uncommon charm of the Caribbean, with its golden beaches, sapphire skies and its waters ever changing in shades depending on time of day and night and weather, was greatly magnified because of your presence."

"Your love is the rudder that keeps my ship on the proper heading on the sometimes stormy seas of life."

"Life in this world does not offer perfection but love has a way of smoothing the jagged edges."

"Your love is a magical moonbeam that illuminates the mystical wonders along my path."

"Your love is music that soothes, enchants, and makes the facets of life's gems gleam with beauty and thus engender joy."

"Your love is a guiding star that keeps me from wandering off the path."

"Once upon a moment I looked into your eyes, the die was cast and I have never looked back."

"If you were a bird and I was a tree, I would love for you to sing on a branch of me."

"You are as graceful and as sensual as a cello and I desire to learn how to play you."

"This journey is far more fascinating with you as my guide; pointing out all the wonder that surrounds us."

"It is truly a delight to rediscover you each time we get together again."

"Love has numerous facets and you possess the admirable capacity to make them all shine at the same time."

"You have the wonderful ability to retain your childlike sense of wonder and zest for life in the midst of simple and also complicated things, all the while conducting yourself with dignity, class, and loveliness; and that is a perfect recipe for charm."

"Last night you and I sailed on an ocean of stars, and as we went by her, the moon, blew us a kiss."

"I have been to the top of the mountain and I can say to you that there is nothing more wonderful on the other side than I can find right here with you."

"Although I have given you reason to do so on more than one occasion, you have neither judged me nor chastised me nor categorized me."

"There is such a thing as blue love. It is mystical, dreamlike, and subtly enchanting. You have brought such a love."

"To be called "a friend" is a great honour and carries with it a great and most rewarding responsibility."

"Perhaps when you come back, you will bring the sun with you and there will be golden days again."

"Your love has reawakened my sense of wonder at the small yet infinitely important things along this journey of life."

"I was quite lost and hitchhiking on the highway of life when you picked me up in your love machine."

"Your love is a river flowing to the sea of my soul."

"Your love is a rainbow heralding the end of the storm."

"You share my preference for solitude and the peace and serenity of mystical woodlands."

"My most cherished music is that of the symphony directed by your love."

"It is enough just to be with you; magic happens and dreams come true."

"You are at home in mystical woodland places, a friend of elves and fairies."

"You and the love that you have brought me are proof that dreams do come true."

"It is exquisitely magical to glide into the land of dreams as I fall asleep to the song of your love in my heart."

"You are the angel that guards our love from the dispositions of gloom born of my sporadic wanderings into the dark side."

"Your presence dispels the shadows of doubt."

"You dispense wisdom not only through your words but most magnificently through your way in life."

"Like a magic spell, your "joie de vivre" has reawakened my sense of wonder."

"No matter the storm, born of natural or human cause, you always have a rainbow to offer."

"No matter how gloomy the day, you always bring sunshine with you."

"I am your number one fan and you have to know that I am cheering for you."

"In my dream you came dressed in robes of northern lights with wolves at your side."

"You are lovely, a pleasure to be with, and so easy to love."

"I have always believed in fairytales; I simply never thought that I would ever get to live one such as I do with you."

"Your delightful persona is refreshing like an evening breeze at the close of a sultry summer day."

"Deep into the forest of dreams I came upon a charming cottage and when I knocked on its door, you welcomed me in."

"You are strong yet petite and sweet and lovely, the quintessence of woman."

"Like a rose with its fragrance, petals, and thorns; the experience of love often involves enchantment, ecstasy, and misery."

"When I was in a dark place, the angels in heaven decided to part with one of their own and sent you to me."

"The orchestra of your love fills the chambers of my soul with magnificent music."

"You came. You smiled. You conquered... ...me. Congratulations, you little love warrioress."

"You are delicately strong, sweetly persuasive, and therefore seldom wrong."

"You came to me draped in northern lights accompanied by a chorus of wolves and wind."

"You are most in your element with a backdrop of magnificent snow sugared mountains and a symphony of sweet sunshine on the side."

"No matter how gloomy the day, the sun shines in my soul the moment I see your smile."

"My love rides on the storm and paints a rainbow at its fading to herald the quiet and the healing after the chaos."

"My love reclines on a cloud embroidering snowflakes that she lets fall to Earth as drops of goodness and loveliness."

"You have come draped in northern lights, accompanied by a chorus of wind, wolves, and Valkyries."

"You are goddess, angel, nymph, and woman; but most of all you are so charmingly and so uniquely you."

"By the veils of the waterfall, you are one with the wild woods and alluring in the mist like a lovely woodland sylph."

"You dispel the gloom like a ray of sunshine on a dismal day or like a rainbow at the passing of a storm."

"I hear your voice in the song of the wolves and the wind, and your words are hauntingly alluring."

"As I become enchanted by your charms, the world around us recedes until there is only you and me and the moment."

"I easily get lost in the magical maze of your charms and I am not in a hurry to find my way out."

"Knowing you as I do, I can understand how the course of history has been altered by the likes of women such as you."

"Your unpretentiousness plays a significant role in your loveliness."

"You are wonderful at letting me see what everyone else missed in me."

"Come what may, my day will be bright because you are in it."

"It matters not where we are, what we are doing or what is happening around us; I just love being with you."

"Your love is like a candle glowing in a window, beckoning a lost soul from the raging storm."

"In my dreams, you are the presence that makes me wish I would never awaken."

"You are an angel who enlightens my path with the light of your love and keeps me from the dark places."

"Once upon a moment, "I" became "we" and our story ensued."

"You are the star that adorns the tree of my life with your love."

"A life without love is an unfinished masterpiece."

"Your eyes express sentences of love which you punctuate with your smile."

"Once upon a magical weekend, we were really quite alone and not in this world."

"You constantly reveal to me how your love is filled with mystique and magic."

"Maybe you are the melody and I am the lyrics, or it is the other way around; in any case, we are a love song."

"It's just not the same without you near; a lot like a sunless season actually."

"Our love began, not with an avalanche of emotions, but rather like a gentle metamorphosis, like the changing of a season... ...and so it grows"

"You are a pearl of a girl and more lovely than words can tell."

"You opened your heart to me like a rosebud welcomes the sun, and love ensued…"

"Love is a river that never stops flowing although sadly, sometimes is dammed and its flow is stopped by prejudice, hatred and rejection. Happily, its energy is stored waiting for the right moment and the right person to release it and to resume its everlasting flow."

"Your love is the capstone in the foundation of my life."

"I love to live, and I live to love – you!"

"Life is like a dance; regardless of the music, I dance best with you."

"Life is like a roller coaster ride but it is a lot more fun since you came along."

"Love is the most precious renewable resource."

"I am not a dark knight but rather a white knight fighting the shadows on my way to you."

"The sun's in the heavens, the bird's in the tree, the deer's in the meadow, and when you're in my arms, all's well with the world."

"Even though we often have to be apart, I always feel your gentle touch upon my heart."

"If you think you have found true love, cherish it and guard it with your daily life."

"Your presence has the uncanny way of taking a totally nondescript day and turning it into a memorable event festooned with love petals."

"Your kiss is bliss, Miss."

"I miss your kiss of bliss, Miss."

"Once upon a dream, our two paths became one and thus began a fairytale; but this is neither dream nor fairytale although there is a princess and I would be her prince..."

"The loveliness of this radiant rose pales in comparison with the loveliness of you."

"Your love has charmed my inner child to come out and play with yours."

"My love, let us go and watch the scarlet sun set into the silver sea, the golden moon rise into the sapphire sky, and let us search the stars for the next episode of our dream..."

"I saw the flowers along the path bow their heads as you walked by... ...and I heard the trees sigh."

"Your love sails the rough and the calm seas by my side and I am ever so grateful to you."

"You have watered my soul with your love and the desert within it has burst into bloom."

"You are a gem of a girl and I love every one of your facets."

"What do you say you and I take the next spaceship out of here and find our own love planet?"

"The sparkle in your eyes is far brighter than that of any emerald I have ever beheld."

"I am not the only one who weeps when you are hurting; I have seen the sun hide behind the clouds and felt the tears of angels."

"You have dispelled the shadows of despair and replaced them with the light of your love."

"A day without you is like a summer without sunshine."

"The moon will not be shining this night for it is jealous of your charms."

"When I am with you, I can feel eternity... ...and it is beyond wonderment."

"Your love has been a lighthouse guiding me out of the storms of my life."

"My love was a forlorn wild bird imprisoned in the cage of my heart until you came along and set it free."

"I awoke to sunbeams playing in your honey hair and for a moment I was lost in one of heaven's many wonders."

"Although I cannot be with you at this moment, I realize that the same sky covering me covers you also and thus we are under the same velvet sheets and it is just fine."

"Your smile always charms and warms the hearts of those fortunate enough to witness it."

"In a sterile and hostile desert of my life I came upon the oasis that is you and now I bask in a lush garden of fulfilment."

"The loveliness of you makes every moment in your presence memorable."

"How do you express to someone how much they mean to you if words fail you? You show them."

"Let my love be a balm for your bruised and battered heart."

"I have always believed in angels but I never thought I would be so blessed as to be in the presence of one such as you every time we are together."

"Our love flows like a river toward an ocean of infinite possibilities."

"As the sun cannot help but shine, so is it impossible for me not to love you."

"You are the most wonderful of dreams to wake up to and to fall back into."

"My love is drawn to you like the sea is drawn to the moon."

"You have a dizzying effect on me but it's all good."

"Today is a snowflake day for there will not be another like it... ...and a snowflake is a wonder of beauty."

"Life does throw curve balls; sometimes you have to duck and sometimes you just have to catch them."

"Your presence always makes me feel like it is the first day of spring."

"Let us walk under the moon, inhale the scent of night and just let our love flow..."

"I have written so much poetry about you that my muse is starting to look anorexic."

"Go out and look up at the full moon tonight. That man up there will be me blowing kisses your way."

"Come slide down the rainbow of life with me... ...there's a vessel of love at the bottom."

"When they tell me that I am 'just' a child, they are denigrating the most beautiful, hope-filled, and innocent phase of this life."

"Come to Destiny town and meet me at the intersection of Love Avenue and Life Street... ...You won't regret it."

"The mere notion that I might have somehow upset you leaves me faint with dismay."

"This amazing love story will never reach its culmination until you decide to play your part... ...and we both know you're perfect for it."

"You are the exclamation mark on a shout of joy."

"My love is a rainbow and every shade from indigo to ruby represents the amplified intensity of my passion."

"You know you are in love when your heart does a somersault each time you think of her (him)."

"Love is to an anguished soul like a mother's arms are to a distressed child."

"If you are the recipient of love and you do not share it, you are a love miser."

"The symphony of life is a great deal more splendid with an accompaniment of your love."

"Love involves action, not merely words."

"Who will come forth and play the part so this drama can unfold and love may at last triumph?"

"You know it is love when all you think about is giving."

"The only thing wrong with this picture is that you're not in it."

"Your quirkiness and eccentricity only serve to fan the flames of passion and love that I have for you."

"She said a lot more by leaving a bowl of juicy red cherries on my doorstep than if she had rung the doorbell."

"Even though we are apart, it gives me comfort to know that the moon smiling at me is the same one that is smiling at you."

"Since I cannot be with you, I asked the wind to carry my song of love to you."

"I realize that you are a wild flower and thus not to be picked but to be loved and cherished."

"Rather than gold in the pot at the end of the rainbow, I'd rather find love."

"In order for a love duet to enchant, both hearts must be in tune."

"It seems to me that 'romance' without intimacy is a lot like a pizza without the toppings."

"I asked the daffodils on my lawn if you were thinking of me and they bowed their golden heads in affirmation in the gentle breeze."

"If the flowers of love are tended in the garden of your soul, there is no room for the weeds of hatred."

"Your presence on the canvas of my mind completes the perfect portrait."

"When someone tells you they love you and you know they mean it, it is like the first kiss of gentle rain after a long and cruel drought."

"Sometimes you know you are giving away too much of your soul but the love that you feel is beyond your control... ...or so it would seem."

"To me there is nothing wrong with lust if it is sprinkled with a good measure of love. But... what do I know?"

"Love is a playground where innocence waits to be awakened."

"In my search for wonders of this world, I feel very fortunate to have chanced upon you."

"Whenever I hear your voice, a skylark bursts into song in my soul."

"You are the loveliest of gems and it is my pleasure and privilege to discover your facets."

"Love is the poem and you are its theme."

"Love is giving someone your all and expecting nothing in return but when that actually happens, something does not feel right and I suppose that is being human as opposed to divine... ...and I am not a god."

"You are the ultimate gear of my love transmission."

"In this sometimes silly race called life, I am just waiting for your love to catch up with mine."

"I asked an angel to direct a sunbeam at your heart and ignite the flame of love within it."

"She has carelessly closed the curtain of the very beautiful and real drama of love and sadly, I am not certain that she realizes what she has done."

"You had me at that first smile you directed my way."

"It is bittersweet to love someone completely... ...and yet not be sure it is not a mirage."

"Like an insightful artist, you add unique touches to the tapestry that is my life."

"'Love' is just a four-letter word; it all depends on what you mean by using it."

"The concept of my life without you engenders the image of a barren and forbidding place."

"Love offers a glimpse of heaven in this life."

"How many precious gems of love does a heart contain and how many can one keep giving away until none are left to give?"

"Your smile and your charm bring a whole new intensity to the term 'body language.'"

"Love makes the most magnificent music and you are my instrument of choice."

"You have such an enchanting and lovely mystique that even angels are given pause to reflect upon when you happen by."

"Be wise in the things you say to your lover in a moment of passion; he or she may actually believe you."

"You cannot 'manufacture' love. You either have it or you do not."

"Some men seek fancy toys, riches, and power but I am content with the wealth and wisdom provided through your friendship."

"There is no need to put you on a pedestal for you are always head and shoulders above the ordinary."

"From across the crowded room your enchanting smile casts a spell under which I fall most willingly."

"My love, I have always believed in angels but I had never met one in person until I met you."

"I was deep in the darkest shadows of despair when you called me and my soul was instantly bathed in light."

"If you were a daisy among thousands in a meadow, I would have no trouble finding you for you are always the most radiant of all."

"I love you such that mere words can never do justice."

"For those who love and trust and are betrayed, there is no greater pain."

"You are like an enticing apple in The Garden of Eden and I wish I were more like Eve."

"I have this notion that love is an ocean and that my heart is a ship and its destination port is you."

"If you tell someone that you don't love them anymore, you are really telling them and admitting to yourself that you never did... ...and perhaps you don't know what love is."

"I know that it is an urban legend that claims the Inuit have a great many words for "snow" but I do think there ought to be several words to express and to describe the many facets and intricacies of 'love'."

"If you claim to be "in love" and also express boredom or ennui, you are not in love."

"Would it not be a fine thing if the love-starved individuals in this world found one another?"

"Love is the key to the door of healing and entry into the home of peace."

"Let our love be a balm for our bruised and battered hearts."

"My love is a grain of sand becoming a perfect pearl and you are the intended recipient."

"My love is a sleeping volcano waiting to erupt at the magic of your touch."

"The sunny radiance of your smile dispels the shadows of doubt and leaves me basking in your warmth."

"Once upon a love, you came along, and the rest is forever changed..."

"My quest for you was the journey and your love is the prize."

"This unfinished love should have been the best and until it finds closure it will never rest."

"Love is an oasis in the desert of daily drudgery."

"Love is the smile on the face of life."

"There is neither solace nor remedy for the malaise born of love gone wrong."

"There is no healing for the wound left by the dagger of betrayal."

"As love intensifies the ecstasy of joy, so betrayal accentuates the agony of sorrow."

"Love is a bottomless well of sighs both happy and sad."

"Love with its warmth gives hope and you are my love."

"There is neither balm nor cure for melancholy born of love gone astray."

"If you were one among the countless stars in the night sky I would have no difficulty finding you for you are the brightest and the loveliest."

"You are a treasure for which no ransom could ever be paid."

"For all her elegance and beauty, Cleopatra would look rather plain standing next to you."

"No matter how cold and drab, a room takes on a warm and pleasant glow when you walk in."

"If I were a singer of opera, you would be my most cherished aria.

"There is much music in my soul but of all the songs there, you are the one I sing the most."

"I wonder how long it takes before the eyes run out of tears and the heart runs out of love. If the answer is never, then I think I know what it is like to be in hell."

"I saw an angel sadly shake her head as she witnessed the futility of this love."

"Sometimes when I am with you I want to keep you like a precious possession; but you are not a thing and in some small and childlike way, that awakens sadness within my soul."

"I often wonder how I lived before I met you and all these hopes and dreams came to be."

"When we are apart I feel incomplete, like an interrupted dream."

"It has not been sunny in my soul since your absence."

"Your presence dispels the shadows of doubt and casts light in the darkest corners of my soul."

"My love is brightly hued but it would seem that you are colour blind."

"The possibility of your absence loomed on the horizon of my consciousness like a threatening storm and now, I can feel the first raindrops of pain, the first wind gusts of sorrow."

"The curtain has been drawn across the real and lovely drama that was love."

"There is no sweeter lullaby than the sweet sound of your voice welcoming me through the portico of pleasant dreams."

"Love is my movie and you are the star."

"My love is locked in the prison of my heart and I am not sure who holds the key."

"Life without you would be like a desperate trek across an endless desert under a bleak sky of unhappiness."

"Your outer loveliness is only eclipsed by the beauty of your inner self."

"When we are apart and I do not hear from you, my spirit wilts like a fragile flower deprived of rain."

"Oh to be a snowflake and to land and to melt on the tip of your pretty nose!"

"At the coming of darkness, if there is no love, sleep will not bring dreams but nightmares."

"Sailing on the sea of love can be stormy but oh, what a ride!"

"Friendship without intimacy is like a dance without music."

"I often feel my words of love are lost like whispers in the storm."

"Sadly, it seems to me that broken promises and betrayal are never far away from a love story."

"It is sad that some individuals seem intent upon sowing the seeds of sorrow and regret in someone else's field of love."

"Sometimes I feel that the pearls of love that I offer go unnoticed."

"Bruised and battered from betrayal, the broken soul seeks solace in the darkness and seeks the oblivion of sleep."

"Countless sleepless nights and too many tears have left my soul empty; a husk carried off on the winds of sorrow and regret."

"Your change of heart has made the sun ashamed to shine and even the birds have become silent."

"Your choices have effectively silenced the song that was in my soul."

"In the dreary desert of daily drudgery, love is an oasis of renewal."

"Your love is like a rare orchid; a precious treasure that you are unwilling to share, much to my regret."

"You must first learn to love yourself with your shortcomings and imperfections before you can learn to love another."

"Your quirks and imperfections are beauty marks of distinction to me."

"In order for love to grow and to thrive, it must be a shared experience."

"I would like to wrap up my love and send it to you but there is no container large enough to accommodate it."

"Whenever I hear the telephone or someone at the door, my heart leaps for joyfulness; but it sinks into sadness when it is not you."

"After night has fallen, please go out and look to the sky. You will see a travelling star glowing with love's energy and you will know that it is from me."

"You're one of a kind and each time I think of you, there is love on my mind."

"I need you to hold me; to tell me that everything will be all right. Does that mean I'm a child?"

"Love allows me to bask in your presence, to be content to watch you breathe, to wait and be patient."

"I have sent forth my love on the wind like gossamer; I know that if you want it, it will find you."

"Please take my hand and let us begin to write the script of this love story."

"When love awakens, like the spirit of springtime, it plants seeds of hope."

"The sun has given me a gift, a solar halo with rainbow hues; a good luck charm for love that no one can take away from me."

"When you awaken in the morning, I will be gone; and you will heave perhaps a sigh of relief, but more likely a sigh of regret."

"You cannot go unnoticed in a crowd, so radiant is your presence."

"It is good to remember the best of the past but it is even better to live in the moment and make the best of that, so all will be remembered as good."

"Unpretentious simplicity and humility engender compelling grace and loveliness."

"Your holistic beauty emanates from your entire self both spiritual and physical."

"When I open the door and find you standing there, I am left without words and perhaps my feelings are best expressed that way."

"I have a childish fantasy where humanity pools all of its goodness and evil shrieks and shrivels and vanishes."

"The fire of my love, once ignited by your charms, will not be extinguished."

"With you by my side, the waterfall is a maiden in flowing veils; without you near me, it is just a waterfall."

"Your sweetness has brought back to me some of the joyful innocence and wonder that I had as a child."

"Once upon my journey, I met an awe-inspiring you and you have come along."

"In no way do I claim to understand what's happened with you; it just did."

"The day may be drizzly and grey but your presence will provide a kaleidoscope of colour accompanied by dazzling sunshine."

"When I look in your eyes I see the rise and fall of cities and empires, the rise and fall of the waves, the tides, and the sea and the coming of dreams; my dreams."

"I was lost in the darkness of things going wrong when you shone the light of your love and dispelled the shadows in my soul."

"Your aura of confidence and calm is reassuring like a ray of sunshine heralding the end of a storm."

"Your presence awakens the senses and love flows like a gentle stream."

"Your sunny smile provides all the warmth and light that I need."

"I consider it a privilege to be by your side and holding your hand awakens sensations throughout my whole being."

"Your humility makes your wondrous beauty even more apparent."

"We have just begun but take my hand and let us go together to the next milestone on the road of life."

"You are the angel who relit the light of hope in my soul."

"You have a way of exorcising the darkness of despair and replacing it with the light of hope."

"Your love has led me away from the highway to hell and onto the stairway to heaven."

"You are a melody and I love to sing you."

"Your love is a beacon that keeps me from straying onto the shoals of uncertainty."

"You are the most beautiful of songs and I love to intone you."

"You are the inspiration that awakens my imagination to endless possibilities."

"I was wandering on the edge of dark despair when you took my hand and led me back into the light of hope."

"I will serve you my love with a hint of hope, a portion of respect, and a dash of admiration on the side."

"Your love has released my soul from the prisons of doubt, fear, and regret."

"Were I able to paint a portrait of your complete beauty, it would be more famous than any in all the art museums of this world."

"Your love of life is infectious and spreads joy wherever you go."

"Your zest for life is contagious and sows optimism wherever you are."

"If you know you have found true love; it is a treasure; cherish it and guard it with your daily life."

"When one is in love, the petty things of this life matter little and the great ones not much more."

"When one is about to get down on one knee to propose, it is wise to first know where the knee will land."

"You are all the lyrics I need to compose my perfect song."

"Whether friends or lovers, what matters is how the souls are connected."

"We have found one another in the endless saga that is the story of our love."

"Love transforms mere existence into vibrant life."

"Each time an old growth forest giant is felled; humanity's doom edges ever closer."

"Your love is the key ingredient in this recipe known as life."

"Your love is the crowning touch in this magnum opus called life."

"Your love is the pièce de résistance in this banquet called life."

"Your love is the stitch that keeps my life from unravelling."

"Love removes the thorns from the lovely and precious rose that is life."

"I have always believed in love; I just did not know it could be as all-encompassing as the love that I have found with you."

"Love is not blind; it chooses to see only the good and to embrace it, and to nurture it."

"Your aura speaks the language of love and though many cannot understand, I do not need a translator."

"Once upon an exquisite weekend, you opened the door to your soul. My spirit entered and I was moved, awed, and enchanted and a magical time ensued."

"Love can make a seemingly most mundane moment magnificently memorable."

"You are refreshingly unique and interesting; you quite fascinate me."

"I consider myself very fortunate that you see as much in me as I see in you."

"There are some who need to belittle others in order to determine their own worth but they will discover that their value is counterfeit."

"A house is not a home if it does not shelter love."

"When I hold you in my arms, I feel faint with a longing that transcends the physical into the spiritual sphere."

"Singing soothes the soul and enables the spirit to soar."

"Once upon a day in spring, your kiss opened my heart and set free the love within. Thus began our love story."

"Once upon a magical night, a moonbeam lit up your eyes and you captured my heart."

"Your love is like the finest of music that echoes in the chambers of my heart."

"Your lively and lovely temperament gladdens the heart of all those fortunate enough to be near you."

"Your love is like a rose in the snow; a symbol of warmth and caring in a world of cold indifference."

"Your love is the most precious of all the instruments playing in the symphony that is my life."

"You are the loveliest of all the instruments playing in the symphony of my life."

"On the river of life there are many curves. Imagine my delightful surprise when around one of them, I encountered you."

"A most ordinary evening became a night of magical charm when you entered the room."

"It is not a coincidence that when I beheld the most beautiful of rainbows, I thought of you."

"You can turn a seemingly most mundane affair into a most memorable experience."

"A romantic fool, as long as I am with you, I shall remain so."

"When I look at you, all my senses awaken; you are sweet inspiration."

"Along the road of life, there are many bends. Imagine my sweet surprise when around of these, I chanced upon you."

"It is not a coincidence that when I beheld the most stunning of sunsets, my thoughts went to you."

"Your presence dispels dark thoughts like bats to their cave and replaces them with white doves and bright butterflies."

"It is not a happenstance that when I saw the loveliest of orchids, my thoughts were of you."

"In my dream I heard your voice echo through the forest; you were calling me home."

"Your love is an elixir that renders even gods envious."

"You rode into the storm that was my life and put chaos to flight."

"In a meadow of loveliness one flower stood out in beauty and caught my attention, and when I smiled at you, you smiled back at me."

"Rock-a-bye my love, as the moon rises high; close your eyes my love, to my lullaby."

"I am infinitely grateful that you were willing to look beyond the obvious when it came to getting to know me."

"Once upon a cloud, an angel sprinkled stardust, and it snowed on Earth."

"Your love ushered in the springtime and drove away the winter that had taken hold of my soul."

"Love does not allow distance or time to affect its status; it endures."

"Against the backdrop of this love, it is easy to forget the chaotic nature of this world."

"The emerald vale is abounding with love from your friends; their song fills the air."

"May your angels light up your path when times are dark, lighten your burdens when they are heavy, and watch over you always."

"Time is not our enemy; it is a means of transport for the unending journey to forever."

"In many ways the past is an obstacle that prevents intimacy with the present."

"The burdens from the past must be discarded in order for one to go on with the journey."

"I am grateful that my angel keeps me away from the pitfalls along the path."

"The music from the sonata of your love fills my heart with serenity and dispels the shadows of sorrow, doubt, and depression."

"Love is an ocean with tides that ebb and flow and currents that grasp and carry off, ever present and powerful.

"You are an extraordinary comet brightly flying across the scope of my consciousness."

"Once again I have let myself wander into the unknown paths of love and I have cherished every footstep along the way with you, notwithstanding the unexpected outcome which remains unknown."

"Your love is a balm for my bruised and battered heart."

"Broken promises trigger an avalanche of mistrust, anguish, and sorrow."

"A loveless life is like a lifeless desert."

"Love flows from my heart like water from a spring; who will drink of it?"

"When we set sail on the sea of love, it was for unknown destinations and what I wished to be an endless journey. That's what a relationship ought to be like."

"If one wishes to redo their life journey without having the opportunity of changing any of it, that person is afraid of death."

"I have been given the gift of great love to share; I am grateful although there is a painful price to pay."

"When I think of life without you, I feel myself sinking into the quicksand of meaninglessness."

"You do not even seem to realize your reach into my heart and how I am not interested in life without you by my side."

"You asked me to come into your life and get on with the journey and the venture; I accepted and learned so much; but I assumed you meant forever."

"Your words and the feelings and emotions that they awaken paradoxically lull me to slumber like a lovely lullaby."

"A new love is like an elixir that heals past hurts, restores hopes, and fills one with a passion for life."

About the Author

Régis Auffray is originally from Peace River, Alberta, Canada. His parents and all of his extended family are from Brittany, France. He is of Celtic descent. Régis is a graduate of the University of British Columbia with an Education Degree majoring in French and English. He has also done some post graduate work in counselling psychology and obtained a diploma in that field. He took early retirement after 32 years in a career as an educator in middle and senior high school.

Régis feels a "kindred spirit" with the romantic poets and the symbolists but many others - Baudelaire, Hugo, Verlaine, Rimbaud, Lamartine, Frost, Keats, Dickinson, etc.

Régis enjoys writing (although he does not "work" at it but waits for inspiration to come), singing (choir), cycling, walking, hiking, music, movies, reading, nature and romance (yes, he admits to being a "hopeful romantic optimist.")

Régis Auffray lives in Chilliwack, British Columbia, Canada. He is the author of three poetry books. *Tales and Whispers* is his first collection of short stories and personal quotes. For more information, type "Regis Auffray" in your Internet browser